the bones

Michael Prince

Gomer

Published in 2014 by Pont Books, an imprint of
Gomer Press, Llandysul, Ceredigion, SA44 4JL

ISBN 978 1 84851 829 2

A CIP record for this title is available from the British Library.

The author and publishers are grateful for the following
permissions:
    Dylan Thomas, *Under Milk Wood* (Everyman) reprinted by
permission of David Higham Associates
    R.S. Thomas, *You* from *Young and Old (Chatto Poets for the
Young, 1976)* reprinted by permission of Gwydion Thomas
    Benjamin Zephaniah, *Dis Poetry* from *City Psalms*
reprinted by permission of Bloodaxe Books.

This book is published with the financial support of the
Welsh Books Council.

Printed and bound in Wales at
Gomer Press, Llandysul, Ceredigion

Dedicated to Di Prince–
Beth's marvellous mum
and my muse and first reader.

Chapter 1

Ben stood on the pavement. The street was narrow and parked cars squeezed the space. The town was crammed inside the extending arms of its outer castle walls. It was a one-way street, soon passing through one of the narrow arches with only a thin ribbon of pavement for pedestrians. Traffic moved slowly only a few inches from the kerb. Standing still, as Ben did now, was not really an option. Passers-by had to step out into the line of cars to get round him. When a young mother with a buggy came along, Ben stood on the road, causing a jam while she went by.

It was deeply embarrassing. He tried to look as if he was unaware of the nuisance he was causing. No one paid him more than fleeting attention. Even so, he felt ridiculous out there on the street, standing about like a gawky teenager. Perhaps he was gawky, but he didn't want to announce it to the entire population of Caernarfon.

It couldn't last, this anonymity. Any minute he would have to become active, play the part his dad had devised for him. Then he *would* look a fool. Then he *would* be the centre of attention. Till then he kept his eyes down and his hands in his pockets and kicked his heels against the wall behind. All the time he was aware that his attempts to look cool simply made him look sullen and pathetic. It was after school and every now and then he caught a glimpse of a green uniform. There was no escape.

In some other circumstance he might have looked alright. He was out of uniform and the gear he was wearing was his favourite: a short black leather jacket over a white T shirt, a pair of denims and black leather boots. Bruce Springsteen. He hadn't told anyone, but his entire look was based on a picture of Bruce on the cover of *Born to Run* in his dad's album collection. Except Bruce had his T shirt tucked into his jeans, like Americans do. Also Bruce had bushy black hair with curls. Ben's was black but straight. He settled for it short at the sides, longer on top and gelled back. It suited him; he was tall and skinny and, he thought, the look gave him a hint of danger. In fact, he was freezing in his leather jacket. It was April and cold.

A voice was shouting through the traffic noise. Although Ben was expecting it, it still made him start. From a third floor window of the pub opposite his dad was calling his name. 'Ben! Ben!' He looked up, still trying to appear detached, but his dad was already a sideshow. Pedestrians stopped to gape. His dad was leaning out of an open sash window. Soot coated his face and vest. 'Ben! Ben! What the bloody hell are you playing at, Ben?'

Ben tried to look as if his dad was a lunatic stranger. Then he looked further up, to the roof. 'Nothing! I can't see anything!' and he shook his head just in case his dad hadn't heard, and held out his arms in a helpless gesture that said 'It's not my fault!' But he felt guilty nonetheless, as if his performance on the street had contributed to the lack of action on the roof of the Ceffyl Du or, to give it its English name, the Black Horse Hotel.

His dad ran his sooty hand through his sooty hair. A grey halo formed around his head and then he disappeared inside. He didn't do angry but he did do exasperated. Ben knew he would be taking out his frustrations on the chimney brush, pushing and twisting it violently when subtlety was needed to navigate an old flue.

Still nothing at roof level. Nothing from the chimney pot. His dad hung out of the window once more. 'Anything? Can you see anything?' Ben shook his head again and his dad went back inside. He was game; you had to give him that. He didn't give up on things.

There was a pause. Ben stood in the traffic again to let an old lady with a shopping trolley go by. The exhaust fumes gave him a headache.

Then the sound of a heavy rumble and thuds came ominously from the pub. Passers by looked up and quickly focused on the third floor sash window from which a black cloud billowed and began sinking towards their upturned faces. They scurried out of harm's way, speckled with soot. Finally his dad appeared, leaning his head out of the window and coughing violently. The cataclysm inside had no visible effect at roof level. Not one black speck escaped from the chimney.

The traffic was moving slowly enough for Ben to slip through between cars to the twin doors of the pub. The note taped on one of them proclaimed CLOSED 3-6pm FOR RENOVATION. BUSINESS AS USUAL. They couldn't afford to close completely, so his mum and dad were doing what they could before morning opening, and for these few hours in the afternoons.

The pub inside was dingy and old fashioned but it did have some character. Upstairs was basic but liveable. His dad had decided to concentrate first on doing up all the upstairs spare rooms and bathrooms so that the pub could become a hotel again, ready for the tourist season.

Ben was forced labour. He was depressed by the

move to another town and another pub in need of TLC. What help he provided was grudging and given with bad grace. It was hard for his mum and dad and he knew his resentment made it harder, but he couldn't help how he felt.

Perhaps his dad had finally bitten off more than they could chew. He had turned round some desperate pubs in the Manchester area as a tenant landlord, paying rent to the brewery, but he'd *bought* the Ceffyl Du! All the family savings were tied up in it. The only reason they could buy it at all was because nobody else would touch it with a bargepole. Ben wondered whether it would prove to be an entirely different beast – not a black horse but a white elephant. The added complication was that they were in Welsh Wales, a country within a country, although they had not realised this until they arrived. Even his dad's notice was evidence of a lack of understanding: an English only notice. In Caernarfon!

Ben's status as an alien had been made shockingly clear to him within the first weeks of living in Caernarfon. They arrived in late August and he started a week later in year 11 of the local comp. He'd moved school a few times but memories of this first day were particularly vivid.

The school buildings were the usual mishmash,

no higher than two storeys, surrounded by concrete and tarmac, playing fields to one side. Almost all secondary schools seemed to squat on the ground like this, drab and sprawling. Paint was peeling. Any accessible flat roof was protected by lines of razor wire worthy of the trenches.

Inside was a pleasant surprise after the dullness of the exterior: bright lights, crowded corridors, artwork on the walls. He waited in reception. The two women behind the desk chatted to him now and then until the head of year came in. He was cheery as he led Ben across an empty playground to the year 11 block, a prefabricated building that, he was told, 'had seen better days' and was due for demolition. It looked to Ben as if the kids had already started taking it down. He asked Ben if he spoke Welsh, which seemed to Ben to be a very odd thing to ask.

He was taken to a shabby first-floor Maths room to be introduced to his form teacher and registration class. Again everything was welcoming, but the prevalence of Welsh in the brief introductions bewildered Ben. The assembly that followed, *gwasanaeth* they called it, was the stuff of nightmare. Not one word of English was spoken. During the course of it Ben looked at everything and everyone anew, as it sank in that this was a foreign culture as well as a different place.

The day carried on in this vein; officially the school was bi-lingual but the default was Welsh. Some of his classes were in English. Others were in both languages. But teachers didn't always remember, or they explained things as if he was a slow learner. The kids spoke only Cymraeg. When he went home that night, he couldn't tell his mum but he felt like weeping.

After the first week, he was shunted off with five other incomers, two of them Poles with very meagre English, to a centre in Porthmadog for an intensive 'Cwrs Cymraeg' to learn some Welsh. Every morning for five days a mini-bus would pick them up and ferry them there. Others came from elsewhere; a disaffected bunch of incomers except for the Poles, Jakub and Wojciech, who listened in intent silence, baffled but resolute. Ben slouched and looked taciturn but he learned quite a lot in that short week. The civilities in any language pleased him. *Helo. Bore da. Sut 'da chi? Iawn, diolch.* He even learnt a few words in Polish.

That was seven months ago. Ben had adapted quite well, he thought. It was a case of having to.

Despite the 'Closed' notice, the door was on the latch and he could let himself in. It seemed to him that nothing is more still than an empty pub, light filtering through stained glass, the smell of beer and disinfectant. He stood for a second and listened to that silence and then made his way upstairs.

The room in question was at the head of the stairs on the top floor. A room with a flue, Ben smiled. He knew he couldn't just barge in there. His dad had anticipated a lot of mess and sealed it off from the inside as far as he could. The last thing they needed was a fine layer of grime all over the pub. It would take a few minutes yet for the soot to settle. Ben knocked on the door. He could hear the traffic on the street outside but nothing from inside. 'Dad! Dad, you ok?'

'Hang on a minute or two and I'll let you in. Get me a glass of water while you're waiting.' He didn't sound happy. If a voice could slump, his dad's did.

Ben took the opportunity to change into some old working clothes in the interval, then fetched the glass of water and knocked again. This time he could hear his dad pulling away the sealing tape from round the door. He opened it only so far as was necessary to let Ben in and then closed it again quickly. Dust danced in the air. A pile of bricks and rubble spilled out of the hearth.

'Bloody lot came down all at once. Chimney's knackered. A right mess.' He ran his hand through his hair again. 'But that's not the end of it. Look at this lot.'

There were some spare dustsheets in a folded pile

on the other side of the room. On top of these was a pile of bones. They were stained with soot and might not have been recognisable but for the skull that was their centrepiece. There was no mistaking that.

Ben picked up a bone, a piece of arm maybe. There was nothing gruesome about it, nothing frightening. It might just as easily have been a piece of interesting pottery in his hand. The lightness of it surprised him.

'Came down with it,' his dad said. 'There's more in the hearth. No point trying to sort them out now. Don't want to shift stuff twice. We'll put the bricks and stones in rubble bags and we can separate the bones as we go. Start with the big stuff.'

His dad and he filled two rubble bags and the pile of bones grew, and then Ben took over filling the bags while his dad humped them downstairs to the skip out back. It took forty minutes of hard work to clear the worst and separate the bones. Then they shovelled up the dust and soot as carefully as they could, trying not to create more eruptions into the air, and looking out for any last pieces of skeleton. They could tell it was a skeleton; not some bits but enough bones, more or less, for a complete person.

There were remnants of clothing too, black or grey with soot: cotton trousers, a thicker woollen top, both in fragile bits, darned in places, and one leather boot more or less intact. The style of the boot in particular suggested *old*. These things awakened Ben to an obvious truth; a person with a life had worn them.

There was no point in trying to clean the room until the dust settled. His dad disassembled the flue rods and tied them up. 'I'll take these. You get something to put *them* in,' he said, pointing at the bone-pile, 'and bring them downstairs will you.'

Ben could not be so detached about the bones. His dad, he thought, was being matter-of-fact to help Ben deal with it. But the *idea* of the human being they once were inhabited them now, like a soul.

There was a small suitcase on top of a wardrobe in another room. It had been there when they arrived; cardboard made to look like leather, but somehow more respectful than a rubble bag. Ben fetched it, picked the bones up singly with the ends of his fingers and placed them inside and then put the clothes and boot on top. Despite his care there was a musical rattling as he carried the suitcase downstairs.

Out back was a courtyard flatteringly referred to as the beer garden where customers went when they needed a smoke. Ben took the case out there. He covered one of the trestle tables with a plastic tablecloth and began to set the bones out on it as he thought they should go. It took him about twenty minutes. He didn't bother with anything too little, like finger or toe bones, just the main ones: the skull at the top, the broken rib cage below that, then a few vertebrae, the pelvis, then the arm and leg bones. Even allowing inches here and there for what was missing, the skeleton was small - a child's.

His dad arrived at this point, showered and shaved.

'It was a kid,' Ben said. 'See how small it is. I reckon it's old.'

His dad sighed.

'We going to report it?'

His dad sighed again. 'Well, we should.'

There was a pause.

'But we won't.'

Another pause.

'Don't get me wrong, son; I think we should, but we can't. I worked on a building site once and the JCB dug up some bones. The site was shut down for three weeks while they investigated. First the police, and then the archaeologists. Those bones were nothing special. Turned out they weren't human. But we were all laid off without pay. We can't afford that here.' He picked up a finger bone and seemed to examine it before dropping it back. 'It would finish us. You can see that, can't you, Ben?'

Ben was surprised to find himself upset. He shrugged. 'Suppose so,' he said. 'But what do we do with them?'

His dad had evidently given this some thought in the shower. 'We have to dump them, but not anywhere connected to this pub or to us. I've got to open up soon. You'll have to do it when it's dark. Best thing may be put them in a bin-liner and find a skip or bin for them some place. Not in that suitcase; it'll attract attention. And if somebody found a case full of human remains there'd be hell to pay. Not in the sea either because the tide could wash it back in again. A skip is best.' He knew he was asking a lot. 'Do you think you could do that for me, Ben? Get rid of them quietly?'

Ben shrugged again. 'Suppose so.'

'And whatever you do, don't say anything to your mother! I'm not happy about it myself, but it would do her head in. Promise me, Ben.'

Ben placed the bones back in the case. 'I won't say anything.' He carried it towards the back door. 'I'll wait till it's dark,' he said.

Just inside the door by the men's toilets was a sort of utility room with a large sink, and an industrial scale washing machine, no longer in use. It was a general dumping ground for miscellaneous stuff including spare cleaning equipment, like the vac, brushes, mop and bucket. Ben put the case in

18

there for now. It was April. By seven, Ben thought, the night would be drawing in. It was an image he liked; the dark flowing in and out like a tide.

He needed a shower. His skin felt dirty. Rather than carry the dust any further than he needed to, he stripped off outside the bathroom and left his clothes on the floor. The shower felt good but it took a while to wash off all the grime and to make sure the shower itself was left clean. It gave him time to think.

Even before he reached his bedroom, he knew that he would not do what his dad had asked. He couldn't. It was as simple as that.

Chapter 2

If ever any beauty I did see,
Which I desired and got, 'twas but a dream of thee

John Donne – *The Good Morrow*

But it wasn't simple; it was the first moral dilemma Ben had ever grappled with in his life. He didn't steal, he didn't disrespect his parents, he didn't pick on people weaker than himself, but these weren't issues for him; they were second nature. This was different. He *was* convinced by his dad's arguments but it made no difference. He couldn't do it. Even his dad knew it wasn't right. As for his mum, he knew how she would feel if she found out. A dead child would still be a child to her. Saying no to his dad would be easier than keeping it from his mum.

That was the simple bit. But there was no gut instinct to tell him what to do next. The best he could do for now was to move the case behind a stack of crates until he'd thought it through. Meantime, if his dad asked, he'd lie and say he'd dumped the bones. What else could he do?

By morning he'd decided to leave any decision

until the weekend, two days away. School would be a welcome distraction. Despite everything, he liked school. There were problems at first trying to mix and match schoolwork he'd done in England with what he had to do in Wales but, between him and his teachers, they managed it. Year 11 was special. Ever since he could remember, school had seemed to him to be interminable, more of the same, year after year, but now the end was in sight and study had a point. Courses had to be finished and GCSEs had to be prepared for. He was doing ok. His coursework marks were good.

On a one to one basis the teachers were really dedicated. Getting work out of a lot of the kids was like pulling teeth, so Ben's willingness to take advice and to work at home made most of his teachers like him. Nevertheless, during classes in those first weeks he did his best to avoid drawing any attention to himself. In his old school, he wasn't in a single top set but now he was in quite a few. At first, he had gloomily taken this as a sign that standards were lower. After he began to do well and get praise for his work, he changed his mind; maybe the other schools had underestimated him all along. With some reluctance, he became cheery; he was happy at school.

Top sets in different subjects were mostly composed of the same kids. This meant he had to get to know them a little and they him. What he noticed was the high spirits. They were a happy bunch, cleverer than the rest and bound for better things, and they seemed to know it. It was as if they were permanently in sunshine. Most were from middle class homes in the countryside, the sons and daughters of solicitors, teachers, doctors. Going into every class they chirruped like birds. He would have liked to have been party to their conversations, to have shared their confidence and confidences, but they didn't go out of their way to include him in this chitchat, rarely switching to English. Why should they?

He was not resentful, had never subscribed to the paranoid notion that the Welsh spoke Welsh to snub the English. It was such a bizarrely Anglo-centric prejudice and he always enjoyed watching the little dramas play out. Queues were the best places, in the post office, say, or the butcher's. The leisurely conversation in Welsh at the head of the line would arouse strong anti-Welsh mutterings further back. 'They're as rude as the French!' Ben heard one incomer complain; the French being equally bloody minded about speaking French in France.

As it was, Ben's classmates knew more about him than he did about them. It was natural that they asked him where he came from, or how he was settling in. His Manchester roots had momentary brilliance. Most kids had rarely been out of Gwynedd. They were almost as likely to have visited New York as Manchester. But Ben had little to say about the romance of metropolitan life and he followed neither football team, so interest in his origins soon faded. It was harder for him to find out about them. He knew where they came from.

Despite the barrier between them, he looked forward to their company. The girls took pity on him at first and then grew to like him. When they worked in groups or in pairs, they made an effort to accommodate him. English was the subject he liked best, partly because group work happened most often in that class, but also because he was good at it. He had a natural advantage in both language and literature, not because he *was* English, but because he read so much, even poetry. Sometimes he would learn bits of poems by heart.

His understanding of what he read was the best in the class and in his writing he had a style and maturity none of the others could match. They had two languages but Ben's English vocabulary was wider than theirs. His superiority was implicit in what Mr Mullen said to him and the comments he wrote on his work. When the class were asked questions, Mullen consistently turned to Ben last, as if to get the expert view. In English he was the star. Sometimes if a girl needed help she'd ask him.

Haf was his favourite. He had more or less set his heart on her. This, at least, was how he saw it, and the kind of language in which he rehearsed it. She was his Juliet, 'my set text,' he mused devotedly. He empathised entirely with Romeo's unrequited love at the start of the play, even if it was for the wrong girl. Ben had newly discovered that this was what love did to you. Meanwhile Haf was a picture of blithe indifference. A relationship with him was very definitely 'an honour she thought not of'.

He'd been out with a few girls in Manchester but none since arriving in Caernarfon. On each occasion it had not really been his choice. Each one had made it clear *she* wanted to go out with *him*. He was aware that he was considered quite a prize, but they soon grew bored. Hanging about was not something he enjoyed, even with a girl. He held back from doing much more than kissing because he didn't entirely know how to go about it, but also to avoid anything that suggested interest. Quite early in these liaisons his main preoccupation had been how to escape them.

Haf was different. He picked her out in the early weeks of school. Lots of the girls in top set were pretty, just as most of the lads were tall. It seemed unfair really. But Haf seemed to him to be set apart by her dark eyes and hair. When she was quiet and thoughtful, she seemed entirely detached and serene, but she was also one of the central figures in the group, full of mischief and enthusiasm. Ben would listen to her tell her stories, understanding barely a word, but watching her eyes flash and the drama of her movements. She wore a subtle perfume. Her skin was the colour of ivory, darkening into the recesses of her clothing. He was all but paralysed when she was close. At a distance he longed to be near.

She had no boyfriend in school as far as he knew. She could often be seen arm in arm with her girlfriends. She was never alone. He knew she worked in her village chip shop but, of the rest of her life, Ben knew nothing. At night she boarded the Nantglas bus and was gone.

He looked her up on Facebook. There was surprisingly little, most of it banal chit chat and poor quality photos. No close up, no phone number. There seemed to be no opportunities to develop any relationship with her.

But the day after the bones came down the chimney, it turned out, was a chance. He was partnered with her for a speaking and listening task in English; a brief scene from *Under Milk Wood* to deliver to the class and then they had to give a little tutorial on how they had interpreted the scene and their characters. A double lesson to practise and discuss and make notes and then they had to do it. He was sure they'd been paired because they had been the most dramatic during the class readings of the text. It was a comic scene but, *'with strong sexual undertones'*, as Mr Mullen put it. According to Mullen, the play was all about sex and death.

Pairs spread out in the class and into the corridor outside. Only four pairs were scheduled for the next day and it was these, including Ben and Haf, who took it most seriously. There was still time to improve marks. For Ben it was a godsend. Despite his flat Manchester vowels, he could mimic accents. He loved the lilt of the South Wales voices in the play. After he arrived in Caernarfon, it was one of his first disappointments that the language was everywhere but the musical cadence of South Wales was missing.

Mr Mullen played them an extract from the original radio broadcast, *a play for voices*, with Richard Burton narrating:

To begin at the beginning. It is spring, moonless night in the small town, starless and bible-black …

The sound was everything and Ben loved it.

They carried two chairs to an alcove in the corridor and sat opposite each other. There was another pair quite near them so Ben and Haf had to sit close to each other in order to hear. His legs were too long. It was hard not to touch knees. Even with a gap between them, he was sure he could feel the heat of her skin next to his. The book shook in his hand.

There were two parts: Mog Edwards (*a draper mad with love*) and Myfanwy Price, his untouchable beloved. But, this being a radio play, there was also a narrator. Haf suggested that Ben do that as well but in the end they agreed to share the role. He began in his best Richard Burton voice and Haf smiled her appreciation. When she read, it was clear that she was doing her best to match him. Almost at once it was a playful competition to see who could outdo the other for melodrama and comic effects.

BEN   *From where you are, you can hear, in Cockle Row in the spring, moonless night, Miss Price, dressmaker and sweetshop-keeper, dream of*

HAF   *her lover, tall as a town clock tower, Samson-syrup-gold-maned, whacking thighed and piping hot …*

As they read, it came home that it was true; it was all about sex. Ben looked down at the page when he described *her lonely loving hotwaterbottled body* but when he looked up she was smiling again. From then on they threw themselves into it.

MOG *I will warm the sheets like an electric toaster, I will lie by your side like the Sunday roast.*

27

The end of the scene was the tricky bit. Up until then Mog had most of the lines with the 'sexual undertones' but they knew, because Mr Mullen had said so, that Myfanwy's final exclamations were meant to suggest sexual excitement.

MOG   *Myfanwy, Myfanwy, before the mice gnaw at your bottom drawer will you say*

MYFANWY *Yes, Mog, yes, Mog, yes, yes, yes …*

For the first time she was self-conscious. Her words came out flat and dead. Ben gave her a rueful look. 'I think you have to be a bit more excited or else it won't work.'

She took a deep breath and nodded. He read his lines again as passionately as he could and she responded with such wild abandon that the nearby pair stopped and looked.

Yes, Mog, yes, Mog, yes, yes, yes!

'I think that might do it,' he said, and she laughed.

There was a bond between them now and they swapped ideas about the talk that would accompany the performance. It was pleasing to them to be able to praise the other's ideas, a new experience for both of them, as intimate as holding hands but richer. At the end of the lesson they thanked each other.

The formality was another sign that something significant had happened.

The next day they performed for the class. There was a hushed silence as they acted the scene, followed by raucous applause. No other pair was prepared to throw itself so wholeheartedly into role. The effect was briefly magical. But, under the gaze of the others it was hard to smile afterwards or to look at each other. Their subsequent discussion of the text was a bit cold. The chemistry didn't last. Haf went back to her chair and another group began.

By Friday it felt like nothing had been achieved with Haf. He thought afterwards that he could have asked for her mobile number when they were working together. Now it was more awkward. There was no one else in the class he knew well enough to ask for her number. The idea that other people would know that he fancied her appalled him. Even if he'd had her number, he might not have had the courage to call. He returned instead to unrequited love. At least you could rely on it.

Chapter 3

You go into the street,
And the same world's there:
The same helping of air
As the rich have ...
At the top of a tall tower
The sun stands telling
The time of your life.

R.S.Thomas – *You*

After school on Friday he surprised his mum and dad by quickly getting changed so that he could help them with the redecorating. The dust had been cleared and they were stripping wallpaper. Some rooms had been abandoned, airless and damp for a number of years, and wallpaper was peeling off on its own. Unfortunately there were layers of even older paper underneath. Ben's mum was working on one wall and his dad on the other. There was a technique. No energy was wasted on wallpaper that had not been thoroughly soaked first with a sponge. This was done more than once to make sure it was saturated. It wasn't just water on the sponge; wallpaper paste was added to make it stick to the paper and not dribble down to the floor straight away. This had the unfortunately effect of making everything sticky but it was working. Ben joined his mum and the layers of paper scraped off with relative ease.

His mum was wearing tracksuit bottoms and one of his dad's old shirts with the sleeves rolled up. Seeing her working like this reminded Ben that she was a relatively young woman, only 38. She was slim and wiry, like his dad. Beside Ben she was tiny, her head not as high as his shoulders, but she was tough. Physical labour didn't bother her at all. She was also fearless. If customers got stroppy in the pub she would be a calm and formidable force guiding them towards the door. She could also look lovely even in the scruffiest clothes or, as now, with bits of paper sticking to her face.

Ben could do the parts she couldn't reach and they had the wall done in an hour. Then she helped his dad while Ben swept up, filling bin-liners with soggy strips of wallpaper.

'He comes in handy sometimes, doesn't he, Vinnie?' she said. 'After a hard day in school too.'

'Yep, I reckon we're a good team, us three, when we work together. How many walls have we done in our time? I think stripping has been one of the things that has held our marriage together, eh, Cath?' He winked at Ben. 'And do you know, Ben, she'd never done it before she met me.'

'No, I hadn't. If I'd known then what I know now, I wouldn't have either. I was destined for better things till you swept me off my feet.' She was prodding him with her finger. 'I was going to work in an office and wear smart clothes, and look at me now! Wearing rags, hands worn out by thankless drudgery, and a husband who mocks the sacrifice I made in marrying him.'

Ben was used to their banter. Sometimes his mother's little speeches had a rehearsed quality because she used them with a few variations time and time again as part of these marriage rituals. The end was predictable. His dad would put his arm round her shoulders and she would try unsuccessfully to shrug him off. 'Don't try to get round me like that!' she'd say. 'You've burnt your boats this time!' But his arm would still be round her and he'd give her a kiss.

He was envious of his mum and dad. They were happy together and they could take this happiness with them when they moved. They loved him of course, but there was a completeness about their relationship that he was outside of, like a tangent to a circle. Sometimes watching them together made him wish he had a brother or sister.

They knew it was tough for him, moving as often as they had, and both in their different ways tried to be a pal to him. His mum would always ask him how he was doing and if he was making friends. His dad took him fishing and enlisted his help so that they could work together.

If Ben was lonely, and he wasn't sure he was, he was used to it. Even in Manchester they had moved three times in six years to places a long way apart, so he had no really close friends by the time he left. Anyway, most things he liked were relatively solitary, like reading and cycling, and he was a good skateboarder. Maybe he could get in with a bunch that was into that. Kids into alternative culture might be more interesting. He could not see himself becoming an Emo or a Goth or even a fully dressed skateboarder, but they were gentle, thoughtful types in the main. It was worth a try. At least there was more point in making friends here because the Ceffyl Du was long term; this town was where he was going to live for the foreseeable future.

In this spirit, Ben smartened himself up, and by 7.30 he was on his way to the youth club. It was dark and a cold wind blew in off the Menai Straits and the Irish Sea beyond. His leather jacket was useless at keeping out the chill.

He turned left out of the pub onto the narrow cobbled thoroughfare known, rather oddly, as Stryd Fawr or High Street. It was hardly a main street, but Stryd Fawr cut across the middle of the old walled town within the castle walls and ran from west gate to east gate, the arched entrances through the medieval walls. Four streets ran north to south across it. Each had a different name depending on whether it was north or south of it. The detail Ben liked best was how Stryd yr Eglwys, or Church Street, to the north became Stryd y Jêl – the street of the jail – at its southern end. Shops and houses were crammed in the spaces between. The streets were narrow, cosy and enclosed.

He left the walled part of the town through its East Gate, crossed Bangor Road and headed quite steeply up South Penrallt, a narrow street of higgledy piggledy terraced houses of varying heights, the back entrance to Argos, a chapel and then the youth club housed in a old Victorian school. The words BOARD SCHOOL were picked out boldly in stone high up. In its heyday there had been two entrances in use, one with BOYS carved over the door and the other with GIRLS. The only way now into the youth club was through two high metal doors at the BOYS end. There was a light over the doors. One of them was open. Music came from inside.

Three boys stood by the door sharing a cigarette. They looked as cold as he felt, shifting from foot to foot to keep warm. He'd seen them before, not always together, about town and, quite often, waiting outside the school gates at the end of the day. Two of them he'd seen in school. These two wore sweaters, black tracksuit bottoms and trainers, no coats. At a guess, he would have said they were in year ten. The third was probably in year eleven. He wore a white Adidas tracksuit with red trim, the equivalent of Sunday best for malingering youth in Caernarfon. Ben had seen it often, or ones very like it - grubby on close inspection, frayed at the cuffs, showing stains.

Tracksuit boy was taller than the other two, but was still significantly smaller than Ben. He stepped out to partly bar the door. 'You got a cigarette to spare, mate?'

'Sorry ... don't smoke.'

'No need to be sorry.' He spat between his teeth. 'It's a free country. You don't smoke, you don't smoke.' He moved out of the way.

Before Ben could go inside the smallest boy joined in. 'You're Ben, yeh? Your dad took over the Ceffyl Du.'

Ben nodded.

'It was my uncle Twm sold it. We seen you in school. You came from Manchester, yeh? How do yer like Caernarfon? Bit of a change, yeh?'

'It's ok.' He could only mutter a response. The situation had turned out more civilised than he expected. They seemed harmless enough. 'Yeh, well ... see you then.'

'Yeah, see you.'

He stepped in. They stayed outside.

The first thing that struck you about the building inside was its size. The reception area with its signing-in book was big, and then there were various rooms off. The ceilings were high. It created an immediate sense of space, somewhere kids could spread out. Ben had been twice before. It was the kind of a place that you couldn't put together in your head once you left it.

The next thing you noticed was the colour. The inside walls were covered in a kind of street art: a huge Popeye, Coca Cola, a purple Lambretta, all done by the kids themselves. It didn't seem brash. It had a kind of beat-up, lived-in class. The floors were stripped wood.

At the other end of this room a disco dancing troupe was going through its moves. Ben was impressed by their intensity, how focused they were. They were all girls ranged between about thirteen and sixteen years old. They weren't in costume. No-one bothered them as they sweated away in their leggings and strappy tops to *Single Ladies (Put a ring on it.)*. The chorus bored into his head like a drill. It wasn't Ben's style but they were good.

Off this was another room to the back that served as a kitchen. He ordered a coffee and took a seat to drink it. Two lads were decorating a cake on a work surface. There were rules about food and drink. You couldn't just wander about with it. The kids knew the rules. 'Play up and you're out' was the overriding maxim.

Barry, the youth worker, had given him a quick tour the first time he'd been there. Tall and broad-chested, he looked like a marine in his grey sweater, a commanding figure. He shook Ben's hand on first introduction. As they walked through, Ben noticed how he dealt with kids, talking to them as adults. More like a foreman than a teacher. He never had to ask anything twice.

Downstairs in the basement, the size of the building was more evident. There was a big weights room where Barry oversaw sessions. The two Poles, Jakub and Wojciech, were down there doing lifts the first time Ben was shown round; big lads. They gave him a smile and a nod, which was quite expressive for them.

Next to it was another even bigger room where the kids could kick a ball about and get rid of surplus energy. Barry explained all this with such enthusiasm that Ben couldn't help but be impressed. He had never been in some of these rooms since that first time, but Ben appreciated the breadth of what the youth club offered. It was a warm, generous place, rough and ready but civilising.

Ben knew some of the older ones who came in. There was a full size snooker table and table-tennis.

He played a couple of frantic games of ping-pong with a skinny year ten kid called Jeb who beat him soundly. The disco dancers had moved on to another number. Then he played a long game of snooker with three other year eleven lads. None of them were very skilled, and the contest felt interminable by the time they got to the colours. It was a relief to finish.

Ben went for a cold drink. He knew one of the older girls in the coffee bar and chatted to her for a while, then left. It was 9.30.

Unsurprisingly, the boys who had waylaid him on the way in were long gone. He had expected them to appear inside at some stage but they never did. Banned probably. Surely the club was better than hanging about the streets. He knew instinctively that they hadn't gone home, not all three of them. They'd just gone somewhere else to hang about. They were like fish in a river, idling against the current, waiting for whatever might turn up. Except they lacked the grace of fish and the river ran slow as treacle.

Chapter 4

Lonely and exalted by the friendship of the wind
And the placid afternoon unfolding
The dangerous future and the smile.

Alun Lewis – *To Edward Thomas*

Early on Saturday morning he headed out on his road bike into Snowdonia. It was all up and down but he enjoyed pushing himself hard. The bike felt good under him. Green fields dotted with sheep lined his route and beyond these the mountains. Trees were coming into leaf. He passed through linear villages, one very much like another: terraced houses abutting the road punctuated by redundant chapels, a church, a garage selling only red diesel, another chapel. Between the villages were hill farms and sloping fields. The roads were spectacular, refurbished. New stone walls that stretched for miles on either side were works of art.

On the ride back, he stopped in Nantglas. The square was really just a crossroads flanked by a pub and a chip shop. Another pub fifty yards on was boarded up. A Spar supplied all the other local needs. It was 12.45, and a surprising number of customers gathered around the trestle tables outside the chippy. Folk were out for Saturday drives into the mountains. A posse of bikers in their leathers stood around their gleaming machines with mugs of tea and chips on trays. The two tables inside were occupied by members of a choir off to a recital, already in their bow-ties and blazers.

Haf was behind the counter in a white overall. Her black hair was under an interesting creation, part hat, part hairnet. Ben was unaccountably affected by the overall; finding her suddenly younger in it, perhaps because she was also wearing less make-up. She seemed to be happy in her work, chatting to customers, smiling. Even here she was not alone. One of her friends, Awen, was working with her.

Ben leaned the bike against a lamppost and took his drink from its carrier, sipping it slowly. He wasn't sure now whether to go in and see her. Maybe she wouldn't like it, maybe he'd seem like some kind of stalker. Anyway, he didn't know what to say and he hadn't anticipated that Awen would be there. He was in his cycle shorts and jersey – pretty geeky. In the end he decided to leave, stowing his drink and buckling on his cycle helmet. While he was doing this, she came outside with a tray, gathering stray cups. She was behind him before he realised.

'You're a long way from home.'

Ben turned to face her, aware that his geekiness was not reduced by his cycling helmet.

She also seemed a little awkward. Perhaps she too would have preferred to have been seen in other circumstances, and without the hairnet.

'I was just taking a ride. I was on my way back. Someone said you worked here. I thought I'd say hello.'

She looked amused. 'But you didn't, did you? You didn't say hello. You were off. That's not very sociable is it?' She was making fun of him. 'And I don't work here much. Just Saturday dinner and one night now, because of the exams. I'm quitting soon.'

'I was lucky then,' he said.

'To meet me in my hairnet? I don't think so.'

There was a pause he should have filled. Each looked away.

'Anyway, some of us have work to do,' and she turned back towards the shop. 'Careful on your bicycle!' she called over her shoulder. 'Like the shorts!'

Riding home, he went back over their conversation. Again he had the feeling that a step had been taken but not necessarily forwards. She was more confident than he was. Surely she must know he fancied her. What she thought of him was still a mystery. She was a pretty girl. Who knew how many times she'd brushed off would-be boyfriends who just popped by to say hello or buy some chips?

He pedalled hard on the way back to work off some of the nervous energy. The exertion made him feel alive. Soon his physical wellbeing spilled over into his mood and he was happy. As his dad always said, 'Slowly, slowly, catchee monkey.'

Out of Nantglas, he passed two of the top set lads leaning on a bus stop in the middle of nowhere with their skateboards. They weren't part of the noisy crowd in the English class who sat centrally towards the back. These two sat up front right by the teacher's desk and kept their voices low. They never answered questions unless asked by name. The girls didn't bother with them. Ben was relieved to remember their names, Dewi and Cai, both Jones but not related as far as he knew. This windy bus stop flanked by fields summed them up somehow – outsiders.

They were oddly matched. Dewi was small by top set standards and Cai was a gangling six footer. Ben pulled up and parked his bike.

'How's it going guys?' He could have asked this in Welsh but, if he did, they'd carry on in Welsh and he'd be lost. It happened every time. 'Where you off – skate park?'

'Yeah.' They were suspicious of his interest.

'I've got a board.'

They seemed confused.

'No,' said Ben, 'not with me. At home.'

For the first time they looked more interested than uncomfortable.

'If you're going there now, maybe I could meet you. I've been a couple of times on my own. It's good. But it's better if you've got someone to talk to. You can't skate the whole time you're there.'

They thought this over.

'Mind if I tag along, once I pick up my board?' He didn't want to strike too lonely a note; nobody wanted to get stuck with a *really* lonely person. But he wanted to be appropriately humble. As far as he could tell from brief acquaintance, they were probably used to being patronised; he was careful to show respect.

'Ok,' said Dewi.

'Iawn,' said Cai. 'See you there.'

He left them to discuss what they had let themselves in for. There was no sign of the bus and he was not overtaken by it on the way into town. He had time to stow the bike, change, dig out his board, and walk to the skate park.

Caernarfon was busier than during the week but hardly bustling. The main tourist season was a month away. His mum was serving food now on the weekends and planned to do it all week in the season. Local custom was picking up. As he passed through the pub on his way out, there were diners at three of the tables in the lounge. In the vault, men with racing papers stared at the tv. His dad was behind the bar, just about kept busy serving the two rooms.

'I'm going to the skate park. Couple of lads from school are up there. I'll be back before teatime.'

'You need any money?'

'Nah, I'm fine.'

'Well, enjoy yourself!' His dad was happy that he had someone to meet. Ben knew he could ask for money if he needed it. The question and reply were a fleeting ritual, celebrating for a moment the trust between them.

'See you later!' Ben pushed out of the door and onto the street.

The skate park was in Coed Helen, a recreation ground above the Slate Quay and harbour, on the other side of the River Seiont that fed it. A swing-bridge gave passage across. When a small fishing boat needed to get into or out of the harbour, a warning siren would sound and, after a delay, the bridge would swing to one side.

The park was up some steep steps, hidden until you reached the top. Then it opened out into a wide, flat area surrounded by trees, surprisingly green and well kept. The steps led onto a grassy field and within that was a fenced off picnic area with tables. To the left were a basketball court, the skate park, and further back than that was the children's play area with the usual swings and roundabouts accompanied by an imaginative array of climbing frames, interesting enough to make him wander over and check them out. Beyond these was a bowling green. The whole place looked very neat and looked-after, the swings painted in bright colours.

The skate park was the exception, with its bleak concrete and metal and the ugly graffiti that marked out every skate park he had ever been to. Here and there, someone had taken care, painted something interesting, or at least been inventive with their tag. Mostly kids with spray cans had scrawled their initials or nicknames carelessly on every available surface. With the stark steel and concrete ramps, the effect was of a city in ruins.

But this impression quickly faded. There were lots of kids there, mostly lads, with their bikes and boards, intent on the moves and turns they wanted to perfect, kids who cared about what they were doing. Activity happened in spurts. A group would go at it for ten minutes and then hang out, talking, sometimes poised on the top of a ramp, doing nothing but blocking the space.

There was something life-affirming about it, meeting together, working at something, talking. They swore continuously and spat almost as often, but Ben was heartened by them. It was hard to imagine anyone who didn't, deep down, want to do something to be proud of and to share the experience. Even the kids with the spray cans wanted to be creative; they just didn't know how. Maybe that was why they felt compelled to spoil things, scrawl on posters, tear the heads off flowers.

Back on the other side of the bridge loomed the castle with its massive walls and towers, looking down on the tourist car park that flanked the harbour. A mistake, Ben thought, to have a car park there, so functional and drab next to the castle with all its history, all its ghosts.

The tide was out. On the Coed Helen side, old boats lay beached in the mud of the harbour. Rusty corrugated sheds squatted on the bank. Despite the tourists and the car park, it was a peaceful scene with its sleeping harbour and the imperturbable castle that dwarfed even the four storey terraces of the town. He noticed almost for the first time that these houses were painted in different pastel shades, giving the town a cared-for almost pretty aspect in the spring sunshine. To the left was the sea and Anglesey across the Straits. From this viewpoint the shoreline and green fields of the island looked uninhabited except for cattle and sheep. He could only see one house.

One thing you always noticed about keen

boarders was their willingness to keep trying things till they got them right. This meant lots of falls, lots of bruises. Like the song said, 'Before you learn how to fly, you have to learn how to fall'. Some kids hadn't got that far; they were just getting the feel of boarding by doing carves, arcing curves from one end of a long concave ramp to another. After that there were dismounts and turns and the air, four wheels off the ground. Then it was tricks and lots of pain till you got them right. Some kids moved onto brutal urban stuff like skating on stair rails. They really smashed themselves up.

When the boys finally arrived, Cai was easy to identify, tall and ungainly, as if he was still getting used to his body. They did things slowly, even the walk across. Skate-boarders didn't wear what you would call a uniform. Most kids wore what they hung out in, nothing smart. The prevailing trend was towards baggy – baggy hoodies, baggy jeans, maybe a woolly hat tight on the head. No-one wore a helmet. Dewi seemed to have had an eye on skate-board fashion when he dressed, but Cai wore a brown sleeveless body warmer that made him look like a big teddy-bear on a diet.

'Bus was late. You been here long?' Dewi said.

'Mae'n brysur,' chipped in Cai.

Ben understood what he said. 'I prefer it busy. When you get tired, you can watch.'

'Bit brysur for me ar y funud. I'll wait till it's a bit quieter,' said Cai.

Ben was reassured by the mixture of Welsh and English. Cai was trying but English didn't come naturally to him. His thinking was in Welsh. The compromise that resulted was comfortable for both of them and set each at ease.

'Iawn,' said Ben.

Dewi and he headed for the ramps. Dewi was good on the ground. They spent time in a high half pipe. Both could do verts where the walls straightened at the top of the U shape. They got a real kick out of it.

But Ben wanted to show what else he could do. He did a few carves to warm up, crouching low until he lifted himself for transitions. His board was the standard concave, narrow and tilted upward towards each end. He'd used special tape to create more friction and grip between his feet and the deck. This was essential, especially for the ollie, the first trick most boarders learned before they moved on to the kickflip. At every skate park Ben had been to, there were kids trying to perfect these moves. He remembered when he learned the ollie. It didn't seem possible to defy gravity in that way. Even after he watched demos on Youtube, it didn't make sense.

He couldn't resist showing off. He did a couple of ollies now on a long straight section between ramps, first getting up speed, crouching, and then accelerating his body upwards, increasing lift by raising his arms. Ben had watched scientific explanations, but he still couldn't understand how that rising front foot, not fastened in any way to the deck, could play such a big part in lifting it, then ride the board through the air. He could see why kids would try it again and again because, once you knew it couldn't be done, you had to do it.

The amount of activity did eventually ease off and Cai joined them. He didn't try anything, just perfected his carves. He looked serene as he glided up and down.

Later they sat on a bench, did some people watching, and chewed the fat. Once exams were over, the next step for Cai and Dewi was going to be surfing. Dewi's parents were surfers. His dad even windsurfed. They had a caravan down at Abersoch. 'I've done quite a bit,' said Dewi, 'but Cai's going to have some lessons when the weather's a bit warmer. You can hire a board and wetsuit but it's not worth it really. We're looking on eBay for Cai's stuff. Dad'll check it out for him. You fancy it? We'll look out for some for you. It's cool.'

Cai endorsed the invitation. 'The trouble sometimes might be getting to the beach but our parents are pretty good. We could squeeze you in.'

'My folks are good too. They'll always give us a ride if we need it,' said Ben. In fact, he had no idea how they could stow surfboards on his dad's jalopy. But in their minds they were there, surfing a crest, sun bronzed, Hawaiian shirts and baggy shorts, or riding in a soft top to a Beachboys' soundtrack. Surfing might mean the Bruce Springsteen look had to go. Win some, lose some.

They reckoned about £120 might be enough to buy the stuff. 'I'll ask my mum and dad,' said Ben. 'You down here tomorrow?'

'Not sure,' said Dewi. 'We sometimes meet here on Sunday afternoon. Depends on gwaith cartref. Other times we meet at Cai's to do gwaith cartref instead.'

Ben couldn't imagine doing his homework with someone else. Thankfully there was no invitation to join them. They picked up their boards and walked into the town centre together before going their separate ways. He thought about how he would ask his parents. The problem was that they *would* say yes. They had little spare cash but they'd do it to make him happy. On the other hand, they were happy when he was happy, so maybe it was money well spent.

Dewi and Cai seemed ok and he did want to be a surfer. He'd grow his hair shoulder length, floppy on one side.

Chapter 5

OK so it's not a bowl of cherries;
still life
must go on.

mp – *Still Life*

On Sunday morning, his mum and dad had a lie in. Saturday night was their busiest but they always did what was needed before going to bed, even if it took them an hour after the pub closed. They would wake relatively late and, when they were ready, they'd shout for cups of tea and the Sunday paper. Between times he sometimes read a book or took a look at his homework. This particular morning he couldn't sit still. It was time to think what to do with the bones. But he couldn't think of anything. In the end he was glad to get the shout for 'Tea!'

Ben delivered it on a tray with all the formality of a butler. They were lavish in their thanks. 'What a fine hotel and what wonderful service, Catherine!'

'You know, Vincent, I don't think I've ever had a finer cup of cha. Shall we have another before we break our fast?'

And so it went on. Ben sat in an armchair while they played their parts. When this was over, his mum was curious about Ben's Saturday.

He told them about his bike ride, but not Haf, and about the skate park. When he mentioned the surfing, the result was predictable.

'When I get time, I'll come down and try it,' his dad said. 'And then me and you, Ben, can get some chicks and surf into the sunset.'

'Your sun *has* set, Vinnie. You haven't got the body for it.'

'What! And he has? There's nothing of him! Six foot streak of nothing!'

'He's a thing of beauty, Vinnie; something to which you've never really been sensitive. But Ben and I *are* sensitive and beautiful, aren't we, love? And we have to stick together, don't we, Ben, because we're living with a philistine.'

Ben liked being in confederacy with his mum. 'Maybe dad'll chill if he takes up surfing, get into the groove.'

'Yeah, groovy, man!' said his dad. 'Who needs beauty? All you need is love!'

'Well, I need breakfast myself, and you to make it, husband of mine.'

'See, Ben, she loves me really,' and his arm went round her shoulders. She elbowed him in the ribs. He winced in mock agony. 'She's sensitive! And I've got the bruises to prove it!' He was getting out of bed. 'Still, what madam wants, madam gets,' and he was on his way to make breakfast.

Ben had eaten. As soon as his parents had breakfast they'd be getting ready to open, working as a team. He had no idea what he would do with the day but he wanted to be out. He needed to think things through, decide what to do.

'Come and give your mum a kiss, Ben!'

She hugged him close. She smelled of sleep and that perfume she wore. 'You're my boy,' and she kissed him. 'Love you.'

'Love you too, mum,' he said, and he did. And that was enough. He kissed her and went downstairs.

His dad was singing in the kitchen. Ben went out towards the back to the utility room. The case was still where he'd left it. He still didn't know what to do.

He took a stroll in the quiet of Sunday morning, turning north for no particular reason, down Stryd yr Eglwys and out through the North Gate. Beyond the town walls, there was a greater sense of space but the buildings seemed more haphazard. Clearly a lot of the buildings that had been there were gone now and redevelopment was only just beginning. A few old places remained: a boatyard; a 1930s cinema, now a bingo hall; a maritime museum, closed, housed in a building resembling a stone cow shed, the whitewash fading.

Outside it on a tarmac apron were various bits of maritime history, lying as if some storm had washed them up like jetsam. All had the commendable quality of being too big and heavy to steal: a huge anchor from the shipwrecked HMS Conway; a black propeller; a rusting buoy. To the left was the sea. Buoys in the water, bright green and yellow, leaned at an acute angle in the current as the tide raced in through the narrow channel of the Straits.

Beyond this was Doc Fictoria where yachts were moored in lines against the pontoon landing stages. A leafless forest of masts pointed to the sky, the clinking rigging filling the air with its manic percussions. There were some expensive craft, most with a brash newness. Ben couldn't see a single person on any of them. A sense of opulent uselessness hung over them; nothing like the beat-up skiffs in the mud by the Slate Quay. Ben studied their names: *Carryon, Child's Play, Tequila Sunrise*.

He thought of *Under Milk Wood* and its *dabfilled sea* and he recited to himself in his best Richard Burton: '*Where the* Rhiannon, *the* Rover, *the* Cormorant, *and the* Star of Wales *tilt and ride.*'

On the sea side of the dock, a high wall with a sea-gate kept the ocean at bay. A quaint building on the wall by the gate was labelled DOCFEISTR in big red letters; strangely Germanic, Ben thought. On the land side of the dock were some of the new developments, all metal, glass and wood: the Doc Café and Galeri, the cultural centre. It was past nine but there were few people about.

The sun was still low in the east behind the buildings. It had not reached the dock. As usual, Ben was under-dressed so he was relieved to take advantage of the warmth inside. It was a visit he had intended to make for a while.

Galeri was as modern as might be expected. The atrium was a full two storeys high and off it were various spaces and offices. Somewhere, Ben knew, was a performing space that doubled up as a cinema occasionally. In the nearest room he could see an exhibition of black and white photos. Comfortable suites of furniture were grouped here and there, and a café provided food and drink. Artwork and posters for events filled the spaces on the walls. Even the doors were crafted.

He wandered about, scanned a few leaflets, looked at forthcoming attractions. Eventually he approached the reception desk where a woman in her thirties was finishing a phone-call. She was speaking in Welsh, but she knew by some sixth sense that she should use English when she turned to him. 'Yes, sir,' and she smiled a friendly smile, 'what can I help you with?'

'I was wondering,' said Ben, 'if there is a drama club here … some kind of drama workshop for young people … I mean like me, teenagers. I wondered if there was something I could join.' He wasn't usually hesitant. It wasn't her that made him shy. It was just that this was the first step into the unknown; he was putting himself on the line.

'Because I'm interested in drama.' His mouth felt dry. 'But I've never really done any in school, on a stage or anything. But I think I'd like it, so I want to try. And that's why I came in here … to find out if there's a club or something.'

'Yes,' she said, 'there is a youth drama group that meets … let me see … erm …' She consulted the diary. 'Yes, Tuesday and Thursday nights, between seven and nine most weeks. They do a little production at the end of the year. Very good, they are. Well, there's only been one so far but it was. Very good. Da iawn.'

'Can I just turn up?'

'No, no. You have to sign up, but I don't know if you can now. You might have to wait till there's a place. It might be the wrong time of year to start.' She didn't want to disappoint him. 'But I can give you a number to call. There's no harm in trying is there? Might as well give it a go.' She gave him a reassuring smile. Then she found the number and a name and wrote them on a piece of paper for him. She smiled again. 'You never know.'

'Thanks for your help,' he said. 'You've been very helpful.'

He folded the paper into his pocket and headed for the door. Out of the windows, he could see that the sun had finally made it over the roofs and was creeping across the quayside. The water glinted.

He'd almost reached the door when she called him back. 'Hello! Young man!' She beckoned him towards her. She was quieter, more confidential now, leaning across the counter towards him. 'I've just realised,' she almost whispered, 'I'm sorry ... I should have said ... the drama group ... it's in Welsh only. I'm sorry.'

And he could see that she was. But he wanted to blame someone.

Chapter 6

We have fallen in the dreams the ever-living
Breathe on the tarnished mirror of the world
And then smooth out with ivory hands and sigh

W. B. Yeats – *The Shadowy Waters*

Maybe this Sunday was going to be one of those days. No drama club, and he still had to decide about the bones. Perhaps he should just do what his dad had said after all. It didn't seem right but, in the absence of any other idea, what alternative was there? Ok, he told himself, I'll get rid of them. But not now. Tonight.

He smiled, despite his bad mood, because he knew this was a prevarication. It enabled him to avoid thinking about it for the rest of the day and, when the night came, he was always free to change his mind. It solved his problem for the moment.

Meanwhile maybe Dewi and Cai would be at the skate park after dinner. He headed home to eat and change but he had very little enthusiasm for any of it. Later he might discuss the drama club idea with his mum but now was too soon.

By early afternoon, the day was warm and sunny and he felt better. He picked up his board and set off. The pub was doing well, quite a few people eating lunch. The street was busy too. Despite it being Sunday, most businesses were open for the tourists. There was a strange mixture of shops close by: the sombre Black Dragon Tattoo with its barred windows, an air ambulance charity shop, Clip a Snip hairdressers, mixed in with some upmarket designer clothes outlets and a jewellers, and then an abandoned shop sunk so far into dereliction that it was an attraction. He'd seen visitors lined up before it to take photos.

The four streets at the castle end of the town were busy with diners. Tables and chairs flowed out into the street from the cafes and pubs on either side and most of the tables were taken. Unfortunately, the Ceffyl Du fronted onto a busy road. No chance there of anything al fresco unless you wanted to kill a few customers.

The narrow streets were fairly crowded now. Tourists were pretty easy to pick out from locals; the way they dressed, the cameras. The majority of people were still locals. As Ben walked, it struck him that two sounds characterised Caernarfon: the keening of the gulls, and the sound of spoken Welsh.

Ben skirted the castle, crossed the swing bridge and climbed up to the park. It was in full use. On days like this you could see the value of public spaces. Dewi and Cai were not there but it was early. He went over towards the green area near the picnic tables, sat on his board and leaned against a tree. It was quite relaxing. There were a few people he knew from school but he stayed out of their way.

Half an hour went by. Maybe he should go and come back later, or maybe he should hang on just a bit longer.

He took a spin on his board for a while, mostly cruising the long runs. He was not in the mood to show off. At least while he was boarding he felt fresh, but almost as soon as he stopped he felt hot and clammy. He returned to his previous spot under the tree to cool down. It was 2.30. Five minutes and he'd go home.

Then he saw them sauntering towards him, the three from outside the youth club. Two of them did not appear to have changed their clothes or maybe they had duplicate sets. White Tracksuit wore white trainers, red chinos and a black and white check sweater like a chessboard. They were sharing a cigarette. White Tracksuit finally flicked it away still lit, signalling his role as leader. They had their shoulders back, their chests out, their arms crooked and unswaying; cocky walkers.

'Big Ben,' said White Tracksuit and they sniggered.

Ben stayed sitting where he was and they stood over him. The little one chimed like a clock, 'Dong! Dong! Dong!' and they grinned at each other in delight, shifting from foot to foot.

Ben stood up wearily and picked up his board. He was at least four inches taller than the biggest of them. 'Gotta go,' he said.

'Don't be like that,' said White Tracksuit. 'We was just having a laugh. Can I have a look at your board?' He was already reaching for it. 'Smart,' he said, and he stowed it under his arm. 'We're going into town. Why don't you come with us. It'll be a laugh.'

There was a pause. Then he very elaborately handed the board back with a bow like a peace offering. 'No good to me,' he said. 'I can't even balance on one of them when it's standing still. None of us can. That's weird innit?'

Once again they surprised him. There was something helpless about them. What really was weird was that they seemed to agree with each other in everything. They were of one mind, as they say, and this was remarkable, even if it seemed to be a very small mind indeed. 'Got any fags?' They strolled into town. Now and then the threesome met people they knew but no-one was sufficiently friendly to give them a cigarette.

When Ben headed towards Stryd Fawr they fell

into step. Ben knew their names by now. White Tracksuit was Skids. The smallest one was Dylan but apparently referred to as Dilys without any objection from him. The third was called Sosban for some reason, perhaps because of his strangely flattened face.

Something about these three was fascinating. They were going to the castle, they said, and they could get him in too. It would be a laugh, they said. This was the only reason they gave for doing anything willingly. But by the time they reached the pub it seemed like it might be interesting to find out how they spent their day. Ben had what he might have called a scientific interest in how they idled away their time. At least they would take his mind off the other stuff. The afternoon was getting on. Decision time was drawing near.

So he stowed his board and wandered with them back towards the castle entrance. Still no cigarettes were forthcoming. Dilys found a largely unsmoked butt in an ashtray on one of the café tables. Skids checked the filter for disease and found it healthy enough to smoke with relish. He lit it and took a drag. 'It's a Bensons,' he said. 'Good stuff. You don't get cancer from Bensons.'

Each took a deep drag in turn, savouring the moment, and looking forward to a long and healthy life. Skids again had the honour of flicking the remains into the path of a white haired lady with a black Scots Terrier on a lead. Cigarettes were two a penny to him, Skids seemed to say, and he was afraid of nothing, man or beast. Dilys and Sosban smiled their approval and they strutted emboldened to the castle entrance.

There was a drawbridge across the ditch allowing access to the front entrance by way of a door inside a great arch. Beyond this was a kiosk from where a man in a suit sold tickets. He was not the quickest. Giving change was a lengthy process. The free access the boys promised involved crawling in below his eye-line. Skids and Ben watched Dilys and Sosban demonstrate. They waited until the queue built up, blocking the view of the gatekeeper, then they joined the queue at the back before scrunching down and crawling between the legs of astonished tourists and under his window. Once on the other side, they legged it into the nearest tower.

Ben had to admit that it did have its comic side but he wasn't sure he would find it a bundle of laughs to do it himself. Nevertheless he did it. It set the blood pumping, that was for sure. Skids and the boys had done it countless times. It never occurred to him to ask them why. Because they could, he supposed.

They were inside Eagle Tower, the biggest one in the castle. The narrow winding stairs going up were disorientating and claustrophobic. The effort of the incessant climb made him dizzy. Skids was some way behind. The Bensons did have some disadvantages after all. He stopped frequently to rasp 'Bloody hell' and check he wasn't having a heart attack. Ben could hear him wheezing.

It was a relief to reach the top. A cool wind blew up there. The other two were waiting. They had recovered their breath. 'That was a laugh, eh?' said Dilys.

It was the tallest of the towers on which three turrets were mounted. There were weathered stone figures mounted on them at intervals, one of them just about recognisable as an eagle. Two white flagpoles pointed up into the sky. Looking outward, the sea stretched across to Anglesey and beyond. The Slate Quay lay below. Looking inward and down, Ben could survey the lawned interior surrounded by the great walls and towers that made up the rest of the castle.

Five minutes later Skids emerged. There was a bit of a queue behind him. He wasn't laughing.

Ben took advantage of the view and the fresh wind. From the tower you could see how the castle commanded both the land and sea about it, a massive statement of authority. The other three were remarkably disinterested. Sosban could see his cousin Iolo's fishing boat moored by the Slate

Quay and he spent some time trying to tell Ben which one it was. 'That one!' he'd say pointing towards a whole row of boats. 'No, not that one! That one!'

Ben had no idea which he meant. 'Oh, that one,' he said, and Sosban seemed satisfied.

Strangely, Sosban had nothing more to say about the boat or his cousin. The best he could do was 'I've been on it.' It transpired that he hadn't gone out to sea. 'I think I'd get seasick,' he said.

The other two had never been out to sea either. They took the view that they would get seasick too, and, anyway, where could you have a laugh?

Skids was back to himself. 'If people tried to climb this, they used to pour burning oil on them. You wouldn't try it a second time if you'd been fried like a chip, eh.' They stared down at the drop.

'I could go a bag of chips,' sighed Dilys.

Cultural discussion over, they descended about half way down before exiting onto the walkway that ran along the castle walls between the towers. There was more space here. More particularly there was a small section of walkway that was sectioned off by red warning tape. Inside it was a small pile of sand and another pile of substantial round pebbles and an unopened bag of cement. They were renewing parts of the walkway, using the pebbles to cobble it.

Quite a bit had already been completed. It looked the part – invisible mending.

Skids looked at the other two and smiled. They smiled back and then all three filled various pockets with rounded rocks. It seemed an odd thing to steal.

'What are you doing?' said Ben.

They didn't answer but moved a little way along.

'Watch this!' said Skids and he took out a stone, weighed it in his hand and then threw it towards the water. It arced and then made a splash, too far below to be heard.

'Yes? So?' said Ben.

'Watch those guys fishing.' said Dilys. 'They don't know what's going on. And them tourists. They see the splashes and they're looking and looking for what's causing 'em. It can take them ages to work it out.'

From where they were standing, the sea just beyond the harbour wall was reachable with a good arm. Three anglers stood on the rocks with their rods. Nearby on the footpath tourists were strolling. Each of the boys threw another rock over the parapet and then ducked down. There was a clear danger of falling short with a stone and hitting one of people on the shore, a risk not lost on the throwers, but it only seemed to add to their excitement.

Ben was appalled. They threw again. The anglers

had begun to look around. Some faces turned to stare up in their general direction.

The splashes drew the attention of a flotilla of swans. At first they were at a safe distance, but the commotion and the gathering onlookers probably made them think they might be fed. The next time the boys threw, the rocks splashed among them. The boys were feverish with excitement. 'Woh! See that?'

The next time they threw, one of the swans began to flounder in the water. It flapped its wings furiously but didn't seem to be able to lift its head. 'We hit one!'

The other swans seemed to know something terrible had happened. They beat their wings and threw back their heads and honked pitifully. Some of them drew close to the stricken bird as if to assist but seemed baffled. It was drowning, its neck useless to lift its head from the sea. As it slowly died faces turned once again to the castle walls.

'Bloody hell! Let's go!' said Skids, and they ran as if a starting gun had sounded.

Ben was stunned. He took the steps down very slowly.

He was at the entrance before a general alarm was raised. A group of people, some of them in tears, began to gather there. A police car arrived and two policemen got out. A systematic search of the walls was organised quickly but the guilty ones were well gone, except for Ben.

Nobody suspected him, perhaps because he was on his own, and he walked out into the gathering dusk. Free and clear, he thought. He wondered if the swan was dead yet.

Chapter 7

He had a vision of them put together
Not like a man, but like a chandelier

Robert Frost – *The Witch of Coös*

Ben went home. He walked slowly. He didn't know where he wanted to be. The image of the dying bird kept flashing into his head. They had killed it, but he was complicit in the crime. They were showing off for him. If he had walked away at once, they might have stopped. If he had been forceful, he could have made them stop. But he didn't.

What was he doing with the layabouts anyway? He tried to work backwards through events. Looking back, he felt as if he had sleepwalked into trouble.

He sometimes watched science documentaries on the tv. One that stuck in his mind was about the origin of the universe and about space and time. There were ideas in it that fascinated him and yet just wouldn't fit in his head, like time going at varying speeds and bending, and the universe expanding outwards in a slow-motion explosion.

Thinking now about events, he felt that time had somehow telescoped. It was Wednesday when the bones came down the chimney and it was only Sunday now and his world had utterly changed in five days. His universe had stopped expanding and was moving back inexorably towards him.

What was to be done? He couldn't turn back time. Nothing now would spare the poor creature its last attempts to lift its head, the terror of drowning. If he reported what had happened it would be the other three who would catch hell. Told one way, he was blameless, but he didn't feel it. Nor did he want to be associated with Skids and the others. If he reported them, it would announce their connection with him to the world. What would his parents think? How let down they would feel! The bond of trust would be broken.

Ben was aware that he was thinking of himself again. He could avoid hurting them and make life easier for himself if he kept quiet. For the second time in four days morality proved much more complicated than Ben had ever imagined.

Perhaps they had already been identified. Perhaps some CCTV camera had them all on film. Well, if that was how it turned out, so be it. Otherwise he'd say nothing. Even now Skids, Dilys, and Sosban weren't bad. Pathetic maybe, but not bad. They never meant to harm the swan. What was the good of dropping them in it? They were most likely scared to death, waiting for the police to call.

Anyway, if he reported them, he'd probably be involved in a full-scale feud. He'd heard of those in Caernarfon. Better to leave them be, steer clear from now on.

He had decided these things by the time he reached home. It didn't make him feel any better. The pub opened again at six and it was five thirty. His mum and dad were eating while they had a chance. Ben didn't want to talk to them. He wanted to be on his own.

'Hiya, Ben,' his mum said. 'Did you have a good time?'

'Yeah, great. I had something to eat while I was out. I've got some schoolwork to do. Do you mind if I go up now and do it?'

'Yeah, 'course. Are you alright?'

'Yeah, fine. Just got some stuff to do. Might as well get it done.'

Ben could feel his mum's eyes on him as he left the room. He knew she'd be up to check on him sooner or later. She knew when he wasn't happy but she also knew when to leave him alone for a while.

He lay on top of his bed. When he was twelve, his mum had bought him a retro lava lamp. He turned it on. It gave little light as he waited for the heat to take effect, before the slobbery shapes began their rising and falling.

One issue was clear in his mind. The bones would have to be reported. It was the least he could do, an opportunity to do right without doing any harm. He had not looked at them since he stowed them in the utility room and he thought about them now, alone among the brushes and mops, like bits of broken crockery.

Then he thought of the swan, imagined the sodden heap of feathers and flesh fished from the sea, heavy now, its neck hanging. He wondered if one man could carry a drowned swan. Probably not. And what could they do with it once it had been examined? How would it be disposed of?

It was with this thought in his head that he made his way down to the utility room. The cardboard case was where he had left it. He cleared a space around the sink, put the case on the work surface, turned on the hot tap, and squeezed in some washing up liquid.

There was no reason why anyone would come to the room at this time but he pushed the door shut and was as quiet as he could be. Finally, he opened the case. The bones were scattered, the skull in a corner. Tears came to his eyes as he surveyed them.

Delicately he lifted aside the fragments of clothing, the boot, and then he took the bones from the case one by one and place them carefully in the sink. All except the skull; he left that where it was. The water was very hot and nearly scalded his fingers. There was a nail-brush in a soap dish on the draining board. When he thought he might safely put his hand in, he took a thigh-bone from the soapy water and gently began to scrub it. A greyness had become engrained in it but it looked cleaner for a wash. He picked out the bigger bones first and then felt around in the scummy water for the smaller ones. Some came up cleaner than others. When each was finished he placed it carefully on the drainer.

Now and then he would look across at the skull waiting its turn patiently. The jawbone was missing. He changed the water in the sink, a little bit cooler this time, but he did not immerse the skull. Instead he held it carefully with his left hand and began to scrub it, dipping the brush in the water at intervals. Then he rubbed it down with a clean cloth. Finally he cleared a space on the drainer, and put it there. The eye sockets looked back at him.

He went back upstairs. There was a black linen draw-string laundry bag in his wardrobe. He brought it down and then carefully placed the bones inside it. Then he gave the inside of the cardboard case a wipe down and put the bag inside. Carefully, he carried the case upstairs and pushed it under his bed. Tomorrow night after school he would tell his dad what had to be done and they would take the remains to the police station. It was never too late to do the right thing.

In fact, he did have some homework to do and he spent the next hour or so trying to do it. His heart wasn't in it and it was hard to concentrate, but he did what he could until he began to feel cold.

He was hungry too. Downstairs they had finished serving meals for the night. His mum was cleaning the kitchen.

'Ok, Ben?' she asked again. 'You finished your schoolwork?'

'Yeah, and now I'm starving. Anything left?'

'You sit down there,' she said 'and I'll bring you something you like.'

Five minutes later a plate of chips, peas and steak and ale pie was put in front of him. 'It's what we had left,' she said. 'I've heated it up but it shouldn't be too dry. You just eat as much as you like and leave what you don't want.'

'It looks great, mum,' he said.

'Can't have my boy going hungry, can I? Eat and I'll clear up after.' She touched the top of his head with her fingers.

'Thanks, mum.'

She carried on cleaning. She was mopping the floor by the stoves. As she worked, she sang quietly.

When the lyrics evaded her she hummed. It was the Adele song she liked – *To make you feel my love*. Ben knew that Bob Dylan had written it. His mum didn't care; she just liked it. She had a good voice. He waited for the song to finish before he took his empty plate to the sink.

'I'll just go and say goodnight to dad,' he said, and he gave her a kiss. 'Night.'

'Sleep tight,' she said.

His dad was in the lounge bar. It was quite full. He was pulling pints and there were customers waiting. Sioned, the barmaid, was serving in the other room.

He gave Ben a helpless look. 'Can't stop, Ben. They're thirsty tonight. I reckon it's the bingo dehydrates them,' and he winked and gave Ben his wry smile.

It was a rule his mum had made. She didn't want Ben behind the bar. Sometimes Ben wished he could help.

'I'm fine, Ben. Your mum'll be through soon. Get yourself gone!' He gestured him out of the door. 'Go on! Night!'

Ben was tired. He brushed his teeth at the sink, threw his clothes on the chair and got into bed. The lava lamp was still on, more animated now, the coloured gloops of wax floating up like giant amoeba. He reached across and turned it off. Rest would not come, he was sure of that, but within five minutes he had fallen into an exhausted sleep.

He woke in the pitch black. At first he had no idea why. Then he heard a faint musical clinking like a far off wind chime, except that it came from inside the room. It stopped and silence returned. Light rain tapped on the window. The clinking began again.

Ben sat up in bed, pulled back the covers and sat on its edge. He kept still then, listening. It was cold and he shivered. There was no other noise now but the faint tap of the rain. Perhaps his imagination had got the better of him. He waited again, heard nothing.

Blindly he groped for the switch on the lava lamp so that it tottered and almost fell. It cast minimal light but it was enough. Ben gazed at it until his vision began to blur.

In the darkness, the bones appeared like intermittent lights in space, or like those subterranean luminescences lurking at the bottoms of deep seas. They seemed to swim in the dark. He watched, mesmerised, as they began to find their places and the skeleton took shape. It floated, swaying like a marionette, like those skeletons on strings that parents buy their children. But much bigger and missing a jawbone and a few fingers and toes, the rib cage damaged.

Once it had reconstructed itself, it seemed more visible in the dark. Perhaps the lava lamp brightened as it warmed up. The skeleton swayed like a drunk. Ben dropped his hands to the bed and gripped the duvet as if to prevent himself from leaping up, but he was paralysed, incapable of anything until the bones made their next move.

Finally a bony arm reached out towards his face, a hand with three bony fingers. Ben struck out to knock it away. His hands passed through it but the arm withdrew. The bones returned to their swaying inaction. The eyes sockets were fixed on him.

He was afraid and yet a voice inside him said over and over again, 'This is a dream! This is a dream!' He didn't believe in ghosts. None of this helped. He imagined himself unable to move or speak for an eternity unless he could break the spell now. 'What do you want?' he said. His throat was dry.

The hand reached out again very slowly. This time he made no attempt to stop it. It seemed to trace the shape of his cheek. Ben couldn't tell if the hand touched his skin or if it was the cold chill of the ghostly bone that he could feel. It was odd but it felt human, almost tender. For an instant he remembered his mum's fingertips on his head. As the hand withdrew, the bones began to melt into the dark and soon they were gone.

Ben didn't want them to go. Too many questions

were unanswered and they seemed to have a purpose for him that was not yet clear. He was suddenly exhausted and cold. He lay down and pulled the duvet over him. His muscles slowly relaxed, his breathing became deeper. Perhaps tomorrow night the ghost or the dream would return like Hamlet's father and tell him more. He slept.

Chapter 8

When my father died I was very young
And my mother sold me while yet my tongue
Could scarce cry Weep! Weep! Weep! Weep!

Adapted from William Blake
The Chimney Sweeper (from *Songs of Innocence*)

When he woke on Monday, he had a clear memory of the events of the night. He wasn't frightened. There was no harm in it as far as he could tell. Dream or ghost? He didn't care. He wanted to know the full story. That meant he would have to keep the bones a while longer, at least for one more night. The cardboard case was under the bed. No sound came from it.

He felt strange on the way to school. The experience of the night before made him feel privileged somehow, as if he had been chosen. No-one else had seen what he'd seen. On the other hand, he thought about the dead swan. He knew there could be repercussions. Images of the poor thing floundering, trying to lift its head, kept appearing in his thoughts. His feelings lurched from excited to sickened as the rival memories flashed before his eyes.

He anticipated some dramatic shaming at assembly but nothing happened. He saw no sign of Skids or Dilys or Sosban in the corridors between lessons. Most likely they had stayed away.

Cai and Dewi beckoned him over at the start of the first class. They had some good news on the surfboard and wetsuit front; they'd see him on the weekend. In the next class, Haf's friend, Awen, smiled and said 'Hello again,' very pointedly when he first saw the two of them. Haf just smiled. Otherwise the day went by. He didn't give it his full attention and it mostly left him alone.

When school finished he was a bit late getting out. He'd left his textbook in the Science lab and, on his return, it was not where he'd put it. He was struck for the first time by the chaos in the room, the sheer amount of miscellaneous paper and books he had to shuffle through. Eventually he found it, only just visible on a high shelf even he could hardly reach.

The school was eerily quiet. It could not have been evacuated more quickly if there had been a plague warning. Faint cries could be heard in the distance, a netball practice on the outside courts. Otherwise there was a profound emptiness; the cleaners were strangely absent, the mass of pupils had vanished to the air.

Ben left the building through its main entrance. Skids, Dilys and Sosban were sharing a cigarette by the gate.

'You staying the night?' asked Skids.

'Maybe Big Ben forgot the time,' said Dilys.

'Bong!' sang Sosban.

It was hard to believe, but they gave the impression of having practised this little routine. Skids was in his chessboard sweater. Dilys and Sosban in uniform.

'I'm suspended,' said Skids.

'He's always suspended,' said Dilys. 'They suspend him. He comes back for a day. And then they suspend him again.'

'I don't give a toss!' said Skids, flicking the cigarette away. 'But I wanted to see you. I wanted to make sure you don't say nothing about Sunday.'

Ben stared down at him.

'You better not,' said Skids. 'We haven't told no-one. Anyone else finds out and we'll know it was you told 'em.' He was pointing his finger unconvincingly.

Ben just looked at him. He wasn't afraid. He simply wondered again how he had ever got mixed up with these three. His silence unnerved them.

'We'll see you again, don't worry,' said Skids, and they wandered off.

Ben waited, making a show of putting his textbook in his bag. It could have been worse. Hopefully that was the end of it.

He was about to head for home when someone called his name.

It was Haf, wearing a black coat and a natty red beret. 'Hello,' she said. 'Are you going into town? I'm going to the dentist near the square. You mind if I walk in with you?'

He could never tell if she knew what she was saying. As if he would mind! As if it wouldn't make his day! As they strolled, he thought about the olden days when a courting couple would 'walk out' together. Anyone passing them now might think that he and Haf were such a pair.

'I've been in the library doing some of my homework until it was time. No point in getting there early. One place I hate going is the dentist's. Even the waiting room freaks me out.'

This was something they had in common. The thing they both hated most was the instrument they use to scrape between the teeth. Sharing the same terror put them at ease. Surprisingly, he knew the town better than she did. They walked across the footbridge and down North Penrallt, coming out at Turf Square. Along the way, he pointed out the youth club. She'd never been.

'What's it like to live in the country?' he asked.

'It's alright … a bit boring sometimes, and a real pain to get anywhere at night.'

'You go out much?' he asked, as innocently as he could.

'No,' she said, 'not much.'

It was the answer he wanted but he didn't know what to say next. They were silent for a few seconds and then they got back on track. She told him where her house was in relation to her village. Ben described the amount of work they had to do on the pub. Time went quickly.

'Well, here we are,' she said. 'The torture chamber. Thanks for keeping me company.'

'Good luck,' he said. 'Rather you than me. See you tomorrow.'

It was only a check-up. He could ask her about it when they next talked. Thank god for dentists, he thought.

'You've cheered up.' His mum didn't miss a trick. 'Had a good day then?'

They were emptying the dishwasher. The windows were steamed up. He still had his uniform on, except the blazer that hung on the back of a chair. Normally he would have gone up to change but tonight he wanted company.

'Anything particular put you in a good mood?' and she nudged him in the ribs as he passed with a pile of crockery.

'Careful! We need these plates,' he said. He stacked them on a shelf.

She looked at him intently when he came back, smiling. 'I think it's you that needs to be careful … if it's what I think it is that's filled you with the joys of Spring.' When Ben said nothing, she was sure. 'Who is she then? Tell mama!'

Ben told her.

'She sounds nice. Haf's a funny name … but pretty.'

'It means summer … and she is nice. She's got lovely olive skin and lovely brown eyes and she's quite tall.'

'That's a bit sizeist isn't it!' She stood beside him to show up the difference in their heights. 'It's not the quantity; it's the quality that counts. But time to make your move, I'd say. Neither of you knows if the other one's interested. And you won't know till you give it a try. If she can resist my handsome boy she's got no taste at all. Remember that! She gets you and she's the lucky one.'

His dad came in. He was in a white vest and was drying his hair with a towel.

'Ben's being sizeist, Vinnie. Seems like he prefers taller girls.'

His dad put the towel aside and stood beside her. She was tiny but he was not so big himself. He put his arm around her neck. 'The best things come in small packages,' and he kissed her. 'You've got to be lucky, mind, to get the right one, I know that.' There was a silence. 'I was just unlucky, that's all.' He dodged out of harm's way before she could punch him and then she chased him round the kitchen.

'Don't you ever sell yourself short, Ben,' she said, and she added loudly, 'not like I did!'

Once again, Ben left them to it. He had schoolwork to do that he might normally have finished over the weekend. Pretty soon school would finish and revising would be the order of the day. Changes came thick and fast these days.

A couple of hours later and the work was done. He went into the family lounge, sprawled on the sofa and flicked through the channels on the tv. In the end he settled for an old episode of *Morse*. Morse, the detective who played opera and drank real ale. Ben had never heard a conversation about opera in any pub they had ever run. But he liked Morse. There were lots of things about people that Morse didn't understand; that was why Morse was lonely and never got the girl. They were all a bit too young for him anyway, the women, Ben thought.

In this episode she turned out to be the killer.

'Sorry, Morse,' she said as she was put in the back seat of the police car. 'If I'd met you sooner … The timing was wrong.' Morse went home, poured a big glass of whiskey and put on some opera. Ben thought that he would have been better with Adele and *To make you feel my love.*

He went down then and said goodnight.

'Night, love,' said his mum. 'Have a good night's sleep.'

He was strangely calm. He got ready for bed and climbed in. It was cold at first. The bones were under the bed. He lay on his back and waited. Soon he was asleep.

He woke to the wind-chime music, lay there listening for a while before turning on the lamp. The bones were already assembled, swaying. Ben sat up and then automatically took his customary position on the edge of the bed. His feet were cold. The bones swayed and waited.

'What do you want?' Ben said again, helplessly.

'Osian 'dw i.'

Ben started. He had not expected an answer. He said out loud, 'This is a dream!'

'My name is Osian.'

It was a child's voice. A young boy. In the dream, the child spoke in Welsh. Ben could hear it in Welsh and yet understand every word. In the dream it was normal. It was weird, he thought, but it was no weirder than a skeleton that reassembled itself and spoke. 'Anything goes in a dream,' Ben told himself with such remarkable calmness that he wondered uselessly whether he was dreaming of himself dreaming.

The voice stopped. Ben was at a loss, as if there was something he should have known but didn't. Flesh grew on the bones. Ben watched in horror as a child took shape. It was a skinny, sickly-looking boy in a patched woollen top and cotton trousers. There was a deep cut on his head, his hair clotted with blood, and anywhere his skin was exposed there were cuts and grazes. His fingernails were missing, the finger stumps bloody. His brown eyes looked too large for the emaciated face. The soot on his cheeks was smudged as if by tears. His tattered sooty clothes hung from him. One foot had a boot on it. Ben had to tell himself to breathe.

'My name is Osian,' he said again. 'I come from Penrallt. My father was a carpenter of this town, no more than thirty years of age. My mother was a seamstress. I loved my father. But sickness took him to his grave before his time and we were at the poorhouse door. I was seven years old. I had two brothers and a sister, younger than myself. My mother had to send me to work. So it was I was sold to Roberts as a climbing boy; a father and a son, both grown men, who swept the chimneys of the rich in Caernarfon town and beyond.'

Ben had tried to think how bones had got into the chimney. Interred there in some weird remembrance when the house was built perhaps, or stashed in some cavity after foul play. It had not occurred to him that the bones could have been a child sweep. He had heard about them and he felt certain now that Osian's story would take him to a dark place.

'I cannot tell you when it was. Victoria was queen in London. If I had been fatter I would not have been of use to them, but there was never much flesh on me at the best of times ...' There was a pause as if the boy reflected upon those times, or as if strength failed him.

'And we had meagre food to eat. The boys, as they called us, even the girls, were sent climbing up inside chimneys to loosen soot with our brushes. It was dark as they say hell is, and narrow and twisted. More than once I was in such a squeeze I feared I would be stuck forever. When that happened it was best to wriggle loose, and be sharp about it, because a fire below would be lit to give you speed if you did not. The smoke is worse than the soot in your mouth.' Another long pause.

'Two years I worked for the Roberts family. I had no flesh on me and kept my place when other growing boys were cast aside. In truth, most of us grew but little. We never had enough to eat. We were wracked by coughs, the soot and fumes filling our innards. Two boys sickened and died in those two years, but death was no stranger to the poor in such hard times.'

Ben looked again at the big eyes staring from the emaciated face, the bony wrists and ankles. The skin seemed almost see-through. Despite the flesh on the bone, the boy still swayed unsteadily.

Just then, there was a tap on his door and Ben started. In that instant the child was gone.

'Ben, you awake?' His mum spoke in a whisper so as not to wake him if he was asleep.

Ben quickly lay back in bed and pulled the duvet over him. 'Yes, I'm awake, come in,' he said. He had no idea how long he'd sat on the edge of the bed listening. Dream or not, that much was real; his feet were freezing.

His mother came in then. 'It's one o clock. What are you doing with that lamp on? You haven't been trying to read in that light, have you?' She sat beside him and took his hand. She still whispered. 'You're cold as ice. Are you alright?'

'I just dozed off on top of the covers and woke up cold. I'll warm up now. Don't worry. I'm tired. I'll go straight to sleep.'

'Ok,' she said. 'I hope it's not your brown eyed girl keeping you awake.'

'No, mum, it isn't.'

She gave his hand a squeeze. 'Love you, darlin',' she said, and she turned off the lamp and tiptoed out.

Ben was tired. He couldn't believe how tired he was. He lay for a second or two in the dark listening to the silence and then fell into a deep sleep.

Chapter 9

wishin like a washin machine.

mp – *Wishin*

He woke to a bright spring morning. The gulls were in full voice. He pulled the suitcase from under the bed and looked inside. The black bag was still there. He ran his hand over it to feel the shapes of the bones inside. Tonight, he was sure, he would hear the end of the story and he would know what to do. 'What is it that you want from me?' he said out loud.

Meanwhile, there was still a Tuesday to manoeuvre through. He was bound to encounter Haf and talk to her. He had four classes that day and she was in all but one of them. It wasn't as if she would be surprised if he spoke. A conversation would be expected at some point after their walk into town the afternoon before. This should have reassured him, made him feel less anxious. Instead the pressure was exactly the same. Instead of worrying about how he could ever get to talk to her, now he worried that he must.

What would he say apart from 'How was the dentist's?' and what would he say after that? He could not imagine a single scenario in which the brief encounter did not end as soon as it began. 'Let me see your teeth,' was one of the lines he imagined himself uttering before he curled up and died.

He took extra time in the shower. Afterwards he examined his hair and face and chest in the bathroom mirror. He was skinny. Echoing Osian's words out loud he sighed: 'There was never much flesh on me at the best of times.'

Then he practised some more. 'You survived then? And still got all your own teeth?' How to get away from teeth? How to slide seamlessly from molars to a meander on the beach on Saturday afternoon? 'You know what they say is good for your teeth? A stroll by the sea. Maybe we could meet, get to know each other better, strengthen our enamel.'

He gave that up and sprayed on anti-perspirant generously, gelled his hair and spent five minutes arranging and rearranging it. 'I found my vocation this morning,' he said to her in the mirror. 'I spent two hours arranging my hair to please you, and now I know I want to be an architect. Perhaps I could show my gratitude by buying you an ice-cream on the beach on Saturday ... unless, of course, you have sensitive teeth.'

Perhaps it was better not to think about it.

In school, the chief difficulty was deciding on the right moment. Opportunities were many, going in or out of lessons and on the corridors in between. Perhaps he could seek her out at break and make it more formal. The problem with a conversation in passing was that it would pass and she might think little of it. On the other hand, too obviously seeking her out might seem odd and would expose him again to the laughing eyes of her friends. Her friend, Awen, already regarded him as faintly comic. She seemed inclined to laugh whenever she saw him.

Beneath all these concerns ran his natural tendency to put things off. He smiled nervously and gave her a half-hearted wave the first time he saw her, but after that it was all anticipation and false starts. Each time, something intervened at the last minute to force him to hold back or swerve away. There was always someone with her. He had said nothing by dinnertime.

This terrible paralysis would probably have persisted all day if he had not seen her by the lockers. She was on her own. The locker door was clearly giving her a problem.

'Hi, Haf. You ok?'

'Hi, Ben,' she said as if it was the most natural thing in the world. 'I'm glad you turned up. One of the savages has kicked my door in. It's bent and now

93

the lock won't open. My coat and my lunch are in there.'

Ben imagined himself on a white charger riding to her rescue, but he wasn't very good with locks. 'Let's have a look.' He tried the key in the keyhole. 'Sometimes you do it by just turning it gently. Turn it hard and it sticks. Turn it soft and it sometimes goes round. That's the way it used to be with mine until they kicked it in completely.' He turned the key like a safecracker and by some miracle the catch released. At that moment he felt as if there might actually be a god.

'Oh, brilliant! I've been ten minutes and got nowhere. My saviour!' and she began emptying the locker. 'I can't use it again. It's not safe. Will you help me to carry my stuff? Sir will let me keep it in the form room for now.'

Ben carried her coat, a hockey stick, and a bag of kit. The scent of her perfume was on the coat. She carried some files and textbooks. These are her things, thought the knight, a hockey stick balanced awkwardly under his arm. Fortunately, the room was open and they stowed the stuff on and around a desk in the corner.

'There might just be time to eat a sandwich. Do you want one?'

'No,' he lied. 'You go on.'

And she did.

'Your teeth are working ok.'

She laughed at that. 'I was so hungry … but yes, apparently my teeth are fine. He even gave them a polish. I would show them off except I'm using them right now. You obviously have special powers. First you calm me down before the dentist's and then you rescue my stuff from the savages.'

'All in a day's work,' said Clark Kent, smiling. Then the bell rang and kids began coming in.

Ben was in a different registration class. He began sliding towards the door.

'Thanks, Ben,' she said. 'Next time I see you I'll give you a big smile so you can see my lovely teeth. It's the least I can do.'

The next class after registration was double Science. Their seats were about as far apart as they could be. She turned at the start, waved, and showed him her newly polished white teeth. Then she turned her attention to her friends. He felt helpless, special powers or not. Once again, tentative steps had been taken but he was not sure where, if anywhere, they had taken him, nor would he know where to begin from the next time. Were they now friends?

At the end of the day, he saw her briefly, carrying a heavy bag and a hockey stick, waiting with the Nantglas crowd for their bus. He walked the other way towards town. Somehow, maybe, he could get her mobile number. He could have asked her for it; it would not have seemed unnatural if he had seized the moment when he had it. Now it was too late.

Skids and the crew were on the next corner. Skids wore a garish lime green hoodie. His white trainers were ragged and scuffed. The other two were in uniform. Times were hard; there was no communal cigarette. Ben stopped to hear what they had to say.

'Hi, Ben. What you up to then? You going down town? We'll keep you company. We can have a laugh.'

The tone was so different to the last time they had spoken that the scene seemed vaguely surreal. It took him a few seconds to work out how to respond. 'Nah,' he said. 'I'm going that way but I want to go on my own. I've got things to sort out. I've got stuff to do.'

They looked at each other and shifted from foot to foot. In the interval each of them spat between his teeth. It was a skill they had.

Ben had been half turned as if to go but now he turned fully to face them. 'Thing is, I'd prefer it if you left me alone.' He stopped to give them time to take this in. 'I don't mean any offence, but once was enough. You get your laughs one way, and I get mine another, and that's the end of it. I didn't say anything to anyone about the swan and I won't.

Why would I? But I'd just as soon you left me alone from now on.' He paused. 'You understand?'

It was very disorientating. They were trying to work out whether he was threatening them. He was not sure himself. They said nothing. He took this to . signal their agreement and walked on.

'Stuck up bastard!' shouted Skids from a safe distance.

'Bong!' shouted Sosban.

Chapter 10

Thy portion here was grief, thy years
Distilled no other rain, but tears

Henry Vaughan – *An Epitaph*

That night Ben did some research on the computer. It wasn't hard.

'The age for a chimney sweep to begin working was said to be 6 years old, but sometimes they were younger. A young boy or girl was usually bought from poor parents by a master sweep, and the child became a slave. They had to crawl, often naked, through chimneys only about 18 inches wide, shimmying up the flue, using their back, elbows, and knees. (*There was a diagram*). He would use a brush overhead to knock soot loose; the soot would fall down over him. Once the child reached the top, he would slide down and collect the soot pile for his master who would sell it. The children received no wages.

Children who worked as sweeps rarely lived long. The health effects of doing this work were terrible. They often became stunted in their growth and disfigured because of the unnatural position they had to adopt before their bones had fully developed. Their knees and ankle joints were severely damaged. The children's lungs became diseased, and their eyelids were often infected and sore.

The boys would often develop Chimney Sweep Cancer, a cancer of the scrotum that struck the boys in their teens, painful and fatal. In addition to these afflictions, the boys would sometimes get stuck and die in chimneys for various reasons. The use of child sweeps was not made illegal until 1875.'

The details confirmed Osian's account. In addition there were a number of reports of lingering deaths up chimneys, but none that Ben could find where the body was not recovered. But no doubt it had happened.

The miseries of the boys' existence made Ben feel sick. He thought about the comforts he took for granted and the pettiness of his own concerns by comparison to these horrors. He looked again at the diagrams and illustrations. They sent a shiver through him. Later, as he lay in bed, the images flashed before his eyes.

He woke to the wind chime clinks. Osian was already swaying in front of him. He began as if he had never been interrupted, or as if time was short.

'Two years I worked for Roberts. I was bent like a twisted stick. He and his son were some of the last to use climbing boys like me. We had heard tell of a child sweep called George Brewster. They said that he was sent up a flue in London in a great hospital there and he could not get out. The queen heard of it, they said, and she commanded that they pull down the walls till he was free. They found him five days later. He was alive, but died soon after. They said the queen shed tears for him and commanded there be no more children up chimneys. But Roberts was too far from London to care.

I was here in the inn. Roberts sent me climbing with my brush high up. It was deep in soot in there and hard to climb and it twisted ever upwards. I had no idea how high I had climbed and nor did Roberts below. I could hear his call, very distant, and I began to climb down.

It was on a bend that I met calamity. A stone fell away as I grasped it. It must have been loose already, as was all the brick and stone in that part of the chimney. There was a shifting and then it fell about me. Stone rained down, splitting my head and clattering down on my shoulders. I could do no more than hunch myself against the blows and cuts.

I lost my senses from the crack in my head, I do not know for how long. When I came to I could not move. I was squeezed in like a cork in a bottle. About my head were more bricks. My head was split open.

Even calling out was more than I could do. My first thought when my senses returned was that I could not breathe. My mouth was dry with soot. My throat was raw. I tried to call out but my voice was lost, and I coughed and coughed. But not even this moistened my tongue. It was only by painful trying that I began to swallow and loosen my mouth with spittle. My throat burned still.

When I could, I called out. The dullness of the sound told me the thickness of the stone about me. I thought on George Brewster who was saved but died and I prayed that I would be luckier. I knew my only hope lay in rescue; I could do nothing to help myself. Then I was still, though I had precious little choice in that, and waited on providence. Perhaps it was night already. At daylight they would look for me. The cold seeped ever more into my flesh and bones as I waited.

But they did not come, or I could not hear them anywhere near me. There were many flues and many chimneys. I imagined the queen's tears and the inn pulled down brick by brick to free me. The thought warmed me, but the cold and the aching in my bones soon redoubled. Terror filled me.

They were not coming. I was not brave. I cried out and scratched with my hands on the stones until I had no fingernails. I used the last of my strength, and I cried at last to my mother, my brothers and my sister to pray for me and not forget me. Still they did not come.

How long I tormented myself in this way I do not know but I do not think it was long after that I left behind the sorrows of the world.'

He swayed and was silent.

Ben looked again at the wound, the gashes, the bony hands and feet. 'What do you want now?' he asked.

'Beyond Penrallt, close by the ruins the Romans left, is a church with a graveyard. My father was buried there and my mother. I would be with them; I would my bones were there.'

'How will I find it?'

'There is a great white angel made of stone. My father's grave is close by it. It is a small space with a small stone. In the stone a carpenter's plane has been engraved. He was proud of his trade and mother had it cut into the slate though it was money she could ill afford to lose. She loved my father deeply and would have it no other way ... Take my bones there.' He paused again and swayed, his eyes staring into Ben's. 'Take me there.' And then he was gone.

Chapter 11

What is this dust but flesh and bones?
What are these rocks but milestones.

mp – *Milestones*

Ben sat on the edge of his bed. His feet were like ice. He was exhausted and tears prickled in his eyes. He wiped them away and reached under the bed for the suitcase. The black bag of bones was still inside. He loosened the drawstring and felt inside for the skull, took it out, and held it out in front of him. 'Ok,' he said. 'We've come this far. We'll finish what we started,' and he smiled reassuringly into the bony face before him.

Gently he put the skull back and restored the case to its hiding place. He lay back then and pulled the duvet about him. It was a relief to know the story, released like a guilty secret, and to be able to play a part in bringing some sense of resolution. It was something he had to do, as if he somehow shared the blame.

He still didn't discount the possibility that these were dreams. His research could have provided the material for the story he'd just heard, filled his head with ideas that influenced his dream. Why, for instance, should a ghost care where its bones were buried?

But he knew about family ties. He also felt a debt to all the children who lived and died in misery. Whether this Osian was a dream was unimportant in a way; there were hundreds of thousands of Osians who were real enough. As he lay there thinking, children all over the world were dying needlessly, every minute of every day. To deny this Osian would be like denying all the others.

At least he had a clear course of action. The problem of what to do with the bones was entirely resolved. The problem of how exactly to do it had just presented itself. The first thing to do was to find the graveyard and a grave at least 140 years old. Then he would have to dig a hole at the graveside without being arrested and bury the bones in it. Very simple! But this was what he intended to do.

He made discreet enquiries at school during the day. It was a good reason to approach Haf again. She and he were early arrivers for French and he cornered her while he had a chance. He went about it by a roundabout route, asking first about the Roman ruins. She looked lovely. Her blouse had short sleeves. Her olive skin glowed, downed by light brown hair in the angled sunlight.

'You mean Segontium? It's up the hill. It's mostly old stones. Don't expect the Coliseum!'

The idea of Caernarfon being a Roman town and probably a Celtic settlement before that gave it a new dimension. It had its history as much as London or Stone Henge. True, Ben didn't know much of it, but he was learning. Everyone, it turned out, had his or her own story. Even him.

'Is there a church there with a graveyard?'

'Not there exactly but close by there. Llanbeblig.' She gave him a suspicious look. 'What do you want to know for? You haven't seen the light and got religion, have you?

'How do you know I'm not religious?' He was teasing; the first time he'd felt comfortable enough to do it. 'Maybe I am. Maybe I say my prayers every night.'

'No,' she said, 'I just can't see you being religious. You're too … intelligent.' There was gentle mockery in her voice: 'Or you think you are.' And she smiled.

But she wouldn't be sidetracked. 'What do you want to know for?'

'Can't tell you,' he said, as if it was part of the teasing.

'You're a dark horse,' she said. 'The boy from the Ceffyl Du is a dark horse.' She looked him straight in the face and smiled. 'I'll find out,' she said in a singsong voice. 'That's what my mother always says to me: I'll find out, and she does. And I will too. You watch,' and she turned to her arriving friends.

Ben was transfixed, a boy under a spell. She thought about him! If she couldn't *see* him in one way, it must mean she could *see* him in another! And she said he was intelligent! For a few seconds God was in his heaven and all was right with the world. Then he remembered that she had said he was *too* intelligent. Still, he couldn't help thinking things were looking up.

Instead of going home when school finished, he walked briskly up towards Segontium. The Romans clearly preferred the higher ground. Tall terraced houses gave way on both sides to green fields. The field on the left sloped slightly away and the remains of Roman buildings were laid out across it like a floor plan – Segontium.

A few more houses and then Llanbeblig Church on the beginnings of the downslope. The entrance was set back from the road with impressive wrought iron gates painted black. To the right of the entrance was a large stone store-shed with strong metal doors much graffitied in the usual unimaginative style. From the gates a stone path bore right towards the church. Stone built and solid, it had three distinct sections, each a rectangle with a pitched roof. The first had a square tower rising high above the rest, the second had no tower and the last had a smaller, squatter tower with castellated walls. To Ben's untrained eye there was nothing that suggested it was very old, except perhaps a wooden porch also painted black. There were stained glass windows, but they simply looked blank from the outside behind their protective grilling. The church was locked.

To the left of it as Ben looked was a lawned area that carried on a good way. The grass had recently been mowed. Slate gravestones placed flat in the centre of the lawn made a sizeable square surrounded by a wall of more gravestones, as if the entire plot had quite recently been redeveloped and the recovered memorials tastefully reset. A few more recent war graves were especially well kept, the victims shockingly young. A peaceful, pleasant retreat, it was well done. A pair of magpies hopped about.

Ben was fearful that old graves would be untraceable. He walked the length of the church and round its gable, and the shock of what he saw stopped him in his tracks. This was his first view of the land to the other side of the church, also cemetery, but he had never seen one like it.

The lawn ended abruptly, and beyond it was a swaying green jungle of grasses and tall wild flowers and shrubs and young trees. From this jungle poked hundreds of monuments, some of them leaning at odd angles. The ruins of an abandoned Mayan settlement could not have looked more strange and atmospheric; a Gothic paradise.

It was a huge area, about the size of ten football pitches, maybe more. Just when Ben thought it had simply given way to urban scrub, a cross or a carved pillar rose above the greenery. Thorny briars twined everywhere. Someone had missed a trick; it called out for guided tours.

At first it seemed impenetrable but a few narrow paths ran into it. Ben followed one of these between the gravestones. A litter of cans and bottles indicated where it ran close to the road but he quickly turned inward where the dereliction seemed more profound. Gravestone after gravestone was broken or fallen. Trees grew up through them. The lids of raised grave chambers had been heaved away. Ben could imagine the excitement and fear of the lads who dared each other to shift aside the great slabs of slate. What did they find? They were empty now.

He had thought ahead and tucked a small pad and pencil in his pocket. He took it out now and made an elaborate show of making a sketch. If anyone was curious about what he was doing, he wanted to give the impression of doing some research or drawing. In fact, once he left the perimeter he was obscured most of the time by the jungle about him.

The vast majority of the graves only became visible when he was close by them. These were almost all in slate, engraved but not sculpted. Ben knew about slate quarrying in North Wales. Quite likely some of the occupants of the graves could have cut the stones that made their gravestones. They could even have died of diseases caused by that same slate dust in their lungs. Now and then there was a marble memorial, more resistant to the elements and to vandalism, but they seemed cold. The choice of the rich was cast white stone, discolouring now. Ben noticed too how the proportion of Welsh inscriptions decreased as the gravestones got more expensive.

Of the tallest monuments, the most numerous were pointed obelisks that poked towards the sky at different angles, like ballistic missiles. He checked some of the inscriptions. They were 19th century but seemed strangely modern. The statue Ben looked for was not hard to find among them.

It was a white stone angel with its wings spread, anchored on a wide stone plinth. There was not another like it. The face had taken a battering, most of one wing was missing and the tip of the other, and the surface was stained black in places. In total it must have been ten feet high.

Ben looked at the tangle of ivy and ash saplings and briars like barbed wire around the base. How close was 'close by'? He had no idea. He was more than a little bit irritated. In his experience, ghosts could be annoyingly inexact. Practicalities probably bored them, but Ben was painfully aware already of how thorny the undergrowth could be. The back of his right hand was bleeding and his school sweater and trousers were snagged and even torn in one or two places. How to explain that later?

Yet Osian's plot had to be found, and found now while it was light and he could see. He didn't fancy stumbling about in the dark with a torch trying to find a needle in a haystack.

Apart from abandoning this mad quest altogether, the only sensible method was to work outwards from the angel. Perhaps the plot actually was within a few feet. But he needed a tool, something to cut back the bushes and briars. Some of the grounds were maintained. It was likely that there would be some tools somewhere. He circled the church, stopping to go through the sketching routine every now and then.

There was a squat, stone shed with a slate roof off to one side. It had been padlocked but the hasp had been prized away from the door. A hefty concrete roller leaned against it to keep it shut. Ben hauled it away a few feet and opened the door.

The afternoon sun gilded the dust in the air. It smelled of damp and had an earth floor, mostly bare. No doubt things of any value or usefulness had been stolen or moved somewhere safe. There was a box of plastic plant pots of various sizes, a rake with a broken handle and the remains of an electric lawnmower of antique design. An old spade, very heavy, leaned against a wall. In one corner was a disintegrating plywood box containing various rusty trowels and hand forks. Underneath these was a sickle. It too was rusted and had no cutting edge to speak of but it would be a million times better than using his bare hands.

He took the sickle and the spade outside, pushed the door closed and replaced the roller. Traffic went by on the road but no-one saw him as far as he could tell. He honed the blade on the corner of the hut and some of the rust did come off. As he walked back to the angel he held the tools close into his side, especially the sickle. He didn't want to be mistaken for a homicidal stalker. Or the Grim Reaper, he thought.

The sickle was a help. He used a stout stick in one hand to hold back the thorny tangles and then hacked at them with the sickle in the other. Inevitably there were more cuts on his hands. He worked in the vicinity of the angel, clearing just enough to see what was underneath, but it was hard work. He was breathless and sweaty within minutes.

Mostly he worked hunched down so as not to be seen but there was little chance of that. Hopefully any onlooker would think he was a demented relative of one of the departed. Perhaps he was demented. What else would explain what he was doing? He had a blister on his thumb already.

Then he found it, or he thought he had. It was a small slate stone in a tiny plot just big enough for one grave, also edged with slate. It read:

> 'Yr hwn a fu farw
> *Owen Penant*
> *Ionawr 4 1874*
> *Yn 28 Mlwydd Oed*

Etched simply above the lettering was something that resembled a plane. Osian had given him no last name but he felt certain this was it. There was no mention of other family. Most likely the mother was here too, her grave unmarked because there had not been the money for it. Osian believed so, and Ben wanted to believe the same.

Now he started on a hole. He chose a corner edge. Digging proved impossible. Briars and vegetation close to the ground repelled the blunt blade of the spade. He went back to the sickle, hacking a square outline through the undergrowth so that the soil was exposed. Then he used the spade again. In about twenty more sweaty minutes he had dug a hole only about a foot wide but deep enough for his purpose. He laid the tools down beside it and covered it over with cut briars and leaves. His hands were bloody. There was mud on his face. Wearily, he retrieved his schoolbag and walked home.

By the time he reached home he was desperate to get out of his sweaty clothes and shower. He felt so much better after. He also had a sense of relief that this chapter was almost finished and that he had eventually done something honourable; an old fashioned word, but it felt like the right one for the occasion.

It was almost six. Another one of those time warps, he thought. His mum and dad had eaten. He said he was late because he'd met Dewi and Cai about the surfing. This was only a partial lie. They had talked during the day. Arrangements had been made to go and view some surfing stuff on Saturday afternoon. News of this development was enough for his parents. If he was happy, they were.

He went up then and crammed his homework into the hour or so he had to do it. He dressed in some of his older casual clothes and shoved a torch in his pocket. When it was time and he knew his parents would be at work, he carried the case downstairs and put it out of sight while he told them he was going out for a while. If they asked where, he planned to say the youth club, but both were busy. His mum just gave him a thumbs up. It had been only a week and he had told more lies than ever before. Ben suspected that lying became more necessary as you got older, or seemed to, but he knew there was always a choice. Once this was over, he would go back to the truth. He retrieved the case and began his journey.

Chapter 12

The grave's a fine and private place

Andrew Marvell – *To His Coy Mistress*

He had not gone very far when he began to regret using the case. The problem with it was that it drew attention to itself. At a railway station or an airport, it would have gone unnoticed but in Caernarfon on a darkening April evening it was somehow out of place. Any kind of shoulder bag, even a knapsack, and no-one would have given it a second glance, but a case begged questions. This, at least, was how Ben saw it. He considered going back, but then thought better of it.

Peculiarly, Caernarfon had a bypass that ran almost through the centre of town. It created a barrier between the inner and outer parts of the centre, requiring a footbridge and various ugly subterranean passageways to allow people to and fro. Inevitably these subways were daubed with graffiti and smelled of urine.

Ben was thinking too far ahead. He didn't feel uneasy about the underpass until he reached it.

Once again, going back and then taking a different route seemed unnecessary. He simply needed to be calm. After all, it wasn't even fully dark. A single light shone dimly in the gloom of the subway. The others bulbs had expired. Wind blew through it. A polystyrene fast food carton slid along the floor towards him. Five empty bottles of Stella stood against the wall close by the smashed fragments of a sixth.

He quickened his step. If he could have seen the exit he might have run, but there was a dogleg at the other end. Despite the traffic overhead, the subway was quiet. The musical clink of the bones came from the bag.

He was almost through. As he made the dogleg turn onto the ramp going upward to street level, a bike came down towards him. It was out of control. A boy stood up pedaling and another sat on the seat behind him. The bike swerved from side to side as it approached, the boy on the back screaming obscenities. Ben squeezed in against the wall as they went by. It was **Dilys** and Sosban. Walking behind them was Skids. The tracksuit was back. He looked a bit out of it. His eyes were bloodshot. He walked directly towards Ben.

'Got a cigarette?' he said, only then recognising him. 'Oh, it's you. And you don't, do you? 'Cos you're a good boy.'

Ben could tell he was on something. They all were. He could hear the other two screaming again as they came back and then the crash as they fell off the bike.

A minute or so later they staggered out. All three looked at him. He knew what was coming.

'What's with the bag?' said Skids.

'You running away from home?' said Dilys

'I wouldn't. I ran away once. I came back and no-one 'd noticed,' said Sosban. 'Learnt me a lesson, that did.'

There was a moment's silence while they took this in.

'So what's in it then?' persisted Skids.

Ben clasped it to his chest. 'It's none of your business.' he said. 'It's nothing you'd be interested in, I can tell you that, but the bag is my business and not yours. You understand.' He knew this wouldn't satisfy them.

He wasn't afraid. They were more pathetic than usual. But the case was a hindrance. It would be almost impossible to fight and keep hold of it. On the other hand, he could outrun these three with ease, even carrying the bag, and then take some other route to the graveyard. The way of least resistance! Since they were lined up in front of him, he would double back.

'So, I'll see you boys!' and he ran.

He caught them by surprise but he could hear them behind him. 'Bastard!' muttered Dilys breathlessly, and then there was a dull crash and a fearsome screaming behind. The two pursuers seemed to stop but Ben ran on to the top of the ramp on the other side and then waited, catching his breath. No-one was coming. The screaming continued.

He went back cautiously. It was Skid's voice moaning. He drew closer. In the dim light Dilys and Sosban stood over Skids who writhed on the floor by the prone bicycle. Evidently he had run into it in the dark. Ben remembered the torch and switched it on. Skids' tracksuit was a mess, ripped and blood-stained at his knee and elbow. Skid's leg was broken, bent at right angles, like a snapped twig at the shin. The snapped bone was visible, sticking through the skin.

'O Christ!' said Skids. 'Look at me bloody leg!' He was crying.

Ben took out his mobile, walked the little way towards the entrance so that he had a signal, rang 999, and gave the details. Two minutes and it was done. The ambulance was on its way. He was careful to tell the operator that it was dark in the subway.

Dilys and Sosban looked at him in wonder. All they had said since they saw the fracture was 'Shit!' and then, after a pause, 'Shit!' again. They seemed genuinely surprised when Ben told them that the ambulance was coming, as if they thought Skids ineligible.

'Listen,' said Ben. 'I have to go. They said not to move him. You understand, Dilys? Keep him still and hold on to this.' He gave Dilys the torch and then leaned down to Skids. 'The ambulance is coming. Try to stay still. They'll sort you out. The police are coming too but don't worry.'

They could hear the siren. Skids seemed calmer. 'Ta,' he said and then he bit his lip against the pain.

A police car with its flashing lights pulled up close to Ben's exit. A policewoman went by with a lamp 'Is he in there?'

'Yeah, just in there,' said Ben and she hurried down the ramp and round the dogleg.

Ben carried on up the hill, the case under his arm. It was a longer walk than he thought. Behind him he heard the ambulance arrive. Two paramedics with their bags and a stretcher hurried into the underpass.

He went by Segontium and turned in towards the church. There were no lights. The heavy gates were padlocked but a side gate was open. Luckily there was a moon, no need for a torch. He could see the angel, looking whiter in the moonlight. Locating the narrow path wasn't easy. He stumbled once and went sprawling.

Eventually he reached the little burial plot and pulled away the ivy and briars that he had used to cover the hole. He felt around inside to make sure it was empty and then he placed the sickle in the bottom. Blunt as it was, it was a dangerous thing to leave around.

He flicked open the case and felt inside for the right end of the bag before he lifted it out. He loosened the drawstring and felt inside for the skull. He put it to one side, then he lowered himself onto his knees and carefully poured the bones into the hole. They made their familiar clinking sound.

'Well, Osian,' he said, lifting the skull to face him, 'this is the best I can do. Welcome home.'

He placed the skull gently in the hole. He could see in the moonlight the hole was deep enough. Osian's remains took up little room. There was still space for a good covering of soil. The white face looked up at him. He considered saying a prayer but it wasn't something he could do with any conviction. Being on his knees seemed to him to be enough, so he knelt there for a few seconds looking up at the sky, before he scraped soil back into the hole with the spade. He took care to tamp it down tightly before piling the cut scrub back on top for good measure. All that was left was to pick up the case and lean the old spade by the stone shed. It was a fine night. The moon was almost full. Looking back, the angel looked like a great white bird.

The bins were out for collection on Constantine Terrace. He placed the case beside one of them and walked on. The town looked picturesque below, the lights on, the castle all lit up. Back in the underpass, the bike was abandoned, propped up against a wall. Patches of Skid's blood stained the floor where he had lain. It was 9.30. People were going out. He was glad to be going home.

Chapter 13

Dis poetry goes wid me as I pedal me bike,
I've tried Skakespeare, respect due dere,
But dis is de stuff I like

Benjamin Zephaniah – *Dis Poetry*

He woke on Thursday morning bright as a button, as his mum would say. His hands were scratched but he doubted whether anyone would notice. He told her about the accident and ringing for an ambulance. He didn't tell her he knew the boys. She was proud of him: 'You were very grown up. You did well, Ben.'

When his mum told his dad the story, he was impressed too. 'If you can keep your head when all about you are losing theirs …' he said. 'I'm not sure what comes next.'

Ben knew what he meant. He felt refreshed in all sorts of ways, ready to get on with the rest of his life. This was just as well because the exams were almost upon them. The French oral was on Monday.

When he got to school Haf was absent. Two or three others were absent too. He suspected she was doing some extra prep at home. These clever kids knew how to play the game.

He was ok. His French was good and his mock session had gone very well. Still he worked at it in his free time on Thursday and Friday. His mum and dad made sure he was alright and not getting stressed. Otherwise they let him get on with it.

'I don't care how you do,' said his mum. 'Well, of course I do. I want you to do well and I know you will do well, but as long as you've done your best, we can't ask for any more … If that makes any sense. You know what I mean.' She was embarrassed. Then she grabbed him and gave him a kiss. 'That's my boy!'

By the weekend he needed a break from French. He was due to meet Dewi and Cai at Dewi's at one. Dewi's dad was going to drive them to Abersoch to look at some second hand surfing gear. Since Dewi lived near Nantglas, it seemed natural to head in that direction. He made his mum and dad a cup of tea and chewed the fat with them for as long as he could before they had to get up. Then he got out his road bike.

It was a sunny day. The mountains were clear as bells. The cold of ten days ago had given way to early summer warmth. He wheeled his bike out through the west gate, known as Porth-yr-Aur, the Golden Gate, and strolled along the promenade overlooking the sea on the outside of the town walls. There was plenty of time.

A light breeze blew. Surfing weather, he thought, except the sea was still as a millpond. Swans floated serenely by the Slate Quay entrance. Back in town, business was picking up: the keening of gulls, the sound of Welsh. A Saturday market was setting up in the square. He met people he knew. It was good to say 'Hello', 'Good morning', and even 'Bore da' once or twice.

Finally he mounted the bike and headed out. It was mostly uphill but that meant he could look forward to the downhill run home. The landscape was scrubbed clean and clear and the roads were relatively empty. Even some of the villages looked pretty. Nantglas, unfortunately, was too drab and straggly to ever be called picturesque. It was deserted, too early for the chip shop to be open.

He carried on through and onward towards Rhyd Ddu and Beddgelert before slowing to take in the view. Nantlle Ridge snaked across the horizon on his right, a series of peaks with evocative names linked by a winding path along a steep spine. He had walked it with the school hiking club and remembered some of them: Y Garn; Craig Cwm Silyn; Garnedd Goch; Mynydd Graig Goch. Nothing had prepared him for the scale of it, that path along the ridge, winding like a ribbon into the distance.

To the left, some way off, rose the imposing flanks of Snowdon.

He stopped at this point before the road went steeply down into Beddgelert, dismounted the bike, and caught his breath while he took in the incredible view.

But he wanted to see Haf. After a minute or two he set off back, rehearsing what he might say to her. There was a good chance she would not be working so close to the exams but it was best to be prepared. He would ask her out. If there was no opportunity to get her on her own, he would ask if he could have a word with her in private. 'Can I talk to you on your own for a minute?' or 'Do you think we could talk over there?' and then 'I was wondering if you'd like to go out some time,' or 'If you had any spare time, I wondered if you'd like to spend some of it with me.'

The closer to Nantglas he got, the less plausible it sounded. The exams were another obstacle. She obviously wouldn't have time to date. But he was determined. He didn't even care that he was in his cycling shorts again. He would go through with it.

The chip shop was open when he returned but it was only mid-day. There were no customers inside or out. He could not see Haf. Awen was behind the counter. It cost him some embarrassment but he asked her where Haf was. She was sullen. Perhaps it was the hairnet.

'She's finished. I'm finished after today. We'll be busy studying from now on. Burning the midnight oil ... Not as greasy as this stuff.' She looked around her contemptuously, hot and tired already. It was not the most romantic of jobs. There was an awkward pause. A pile of chips was plunged spitting into the fryer.

'You know, I was really pleased when I got this job,' she said. 'That was only a year ago. I hate it now. Don't you think that's weird; how you can change, just like that?'

She thought about this and played with a strand of hair that had escaped the hairnet. 'I never have chips any more. I can't even look at them!'

No answer seemed to be required and Ben had lost the thread of her conversation.

She twisted the lock of hair round her finger and mused some more. 'Anyway, what did you want her for? Do you want me to give her a message?' she said over the noise.

'No,' he said stupidly. 'I'll catch her again.'

'Ok,' she said. 'Here you go,' and she gave him a small bag of chips.

Ben thanked her.

'Nice shorts!' she shouted after him.

He gave her a backward wave and went outside

to sit by a bench and eat the chips. Then he put on his helmet and climbed on his cycle for the ride to Dewi's. It was a couple of miles **back** towards Caernarfon, mostly downhill, an exhilarating ride. When he was in the vicinity of the turn-off he stopped to check the directions. He wasn't lost. The way was clear. He had done what he could, taken a positive step that could not be undone.

The surfboards were next on the agenda, and then surfing lessons. The idea excited him more now that it was close to becoming a reality. And the exams. He'd work hard and do his best like his mum said. Then he had to find a drama group. There was a new theatre being built in Bangor. Maybe he'd try there. Or maybe he'd get his Welsh up to scratch and go back to Galeri. He'd feel as if he was there to stay then

A car pulled up. A woman driver. Haf was in the passenger seat. Her window was rolled down.

'You can move pretty quick when you want to,' she said. 'Awen says you wanted to see me.' She got out of the car.

She was wearing skinny blue jeans and a tight black top. It took him by surprise for a moment. He realized that he had never seen her out of uniform and without a coat on. She looked terrifyingly lovely.

'What was it about?' she said.

'I was on a bike ride,' he said, 'and I came this way. I wanted to see you.'

The woman in the car was obviously her mother. She had turned the engine off and was looking anywhere but at them.

'What about?'

'Not about anything.' It was too late to back off now. 'I just wanted to see you.' He was aware that he was blushing. At first he couldn't look at her to see her response.

'Oh,' she said. 'I was revising ... and Awen called to say you asked for me. I just thought I'd find out why, that's all. Mum gave me a lift.' She shrugged. 'And that's it really ... I've been revising ... Stayed home Thursday and Friday as well. Did you notice I wasn't in?'

He was looking at her now. 'Yeah,' he said. 'Yeah, I noticed.'

'Well,' she said, 'it's not going as well as I'd like and ... I was wondering if you'd like to come round later and help me with my French.'

'Yeah' he said. 'Yeah, I would ...'

She drew closer and put her finger on the end of his nose. 'I'll call you later then,' she said and walked towards the car.

'Yeah, great,' he said, but then he remembered and shouted after her, 'But you don't have my mobile number!'

She had opened the car door. 'Yes I do,' she shouted back over the traffic noise.

'How?'

'Can't tell you,' she said, and she smiled.

END